Surrender to Seduction

Other Books by Alexandra Benedict:

A Forbidden Love
Too Great a Temptation
Too Dangerous to Desire
Surrender to Seduction
Mistress of Paradise
The Infamous Rogue
The Notorious Scoundrel
How to Seduce a Pirate
How to Steal a Pirate's Heart
The Princess and the Pauper
Once Upon a Dream: Volume I
Tales of Forbidden Love

This book is a work of fiction. Names, characters, places, and incidents are products of the author's imagination and are used fictitiously. Any resemblance to actual events, locales, or persons, living or dead, is entirely coincidental.

Surrender to Seduction

ISBN: 979-8519694070

Published by Zorium Books

www.AlexandraBenedict.ca

Alexandra Benedict

Surrender to Seduction

Zorium Books

CHAPTER 1

London, 1821

Miss Henrietta Ashby admired her reflection in the floor mirror. She twirled from side to side, inspecting the shimmering pink ball gown. It had a muslin overlay with short, puffed sleeves trimmed in lace. The rich color complimented the auburn glow of her hair and the deep brown hue of her eyes.

After a minute, she stilled, cocked her head to the side—and smiled. "It's perfect."

"You look lovely, Miss Ashby," said Jenny, her maid.

But Henrietta wanted to look ravishing. She wanted to look like a woman. She wouldn't wear white, frilly dresses anymore, like a debutant. It was time she took a risk with a radiant, more mature costume. Otherwise, she might never marry the man of her dreams.

Oh, love was such a pesky affair! For four years she'd longed for Viscount Ravenswood, ever since his younger brother Peter had married her eldest sister Penelope. *Four* agonizing years, and still the blasted man thought of her as a hoyden, nothing more.

Henrietta had a mind to clout the viscount for his mulishness. She wasn't a lass of sixteen anymore, but a passionate woman of twenty with a need for one equally passionate man. And if the vexing lord would only stop thinking of her as a spirited chit, she could finally take her rightful place as the next Viscountess Ravenswood. She wasn't getting any younger, didn't he know?

"Now for the mask," said Henrietta.

She went over to the bed, tossed the scandal sheets aside—she'd been reading the juiciest bits earlier in the day—and sifted through the many headdresses, searching for the best match. She soon spotted a venetian half-mask with rose feathers. "How charming."

Her maid tied the satin stays behind her head, and Henrietta took one last look at her reflection in the mirror.

If this doesn't draw his notice, I'm going to scratch out his eyes.

With that encouraging thought in mind, Henrietta thanked her maid, then headed for the ballroom. As she neared the arched entranceway, she squared her shoulders and gazed across the brilliant room and the spirited dancers, searching for Ravenswood.

"There you are, Henry!" cried Lady Ashby. She scurried toward her daughter; cheeks flushed. "Where have you been?"

"I'm sorry, Mama."

The woman fluttered her fan. "Can't you ever be on time, Henry?"

Unfortunately, Henrietta could not. She had a penchant for disorder and a tendency to waver over every decision. Alas, it was not her fault she had such a flighty disposition. Truly, it wasn't. Henrietta was the youngest offspring of Baron Ashby, and, as such, the most pampered of the family. She also served as the baron's surrogate son, thus the nickname Henry.

You see, the baron had a brood of children—all girls! Desperate for a male heir, he had christened his *fifth* daughter Henry, and like any indulgent Papa, the baron catered to his "son's" every wish and whim without complaint. Though there was no property to inherit or title to come into, that didn't stop Henrietta from acting the part of the doted upon son and heir. The only trouble with being Henry was the affinity to do as she pleased without a thought to the consequences.

"I want to introduce you to several eligible gentleman," said her mother. "Meet me in the ballroom in five minutes!" And she set off, piqued.

Henrietta whistled a sigh. The family's annual masquerade was becoming a fast tradition. The third so far, it was first initiated at the behest of Lady Ashby to help find Henrietta a mate. With four sisters already wed, Henrietta was the last of the brood to get leg-shackled. Spinsterhood was fast approaching, and that, of course, put Lady Ashby in near hysterics.

But what Mama didn't realize was Henrietta's determination to resist every suitor save one—Viscount Ravenswood.

"Good evening, Miss Ashby."

She bristled.

Oh, that deep, rich voice! It tickled her skin until she was covered in gooseflesh. It made her heart thump loud and fierce, too.

"Good evening, Sebastian."

Ravenswood was the only one in the family who didn't call her by her nickname. It annoyed her beyond words, his willful refusal to grant her even that small level of intimacy. She always called him by his Christian name, though. He would *not* deny her that familiarity, at least.

Slowly she turned around to confront the towering figure of masculine energy—and let out a little gasp.

Mercy, he was stunning, decked in striking black attire, the white ruff of his cravat set high in an elegant knot. Only his sable black locks were a bit untidy, a stray tress curling over his red satin mask. And that spicy scent of Eau de

Cologne! The rosemary and lemon made Henrietta positively light-headed. Oh, why hadn't she brought along her fan? It was overwhelming, the heat radiating from Ravenswood.

"And how are you this evening, Miss Ashby?"

"I'm very well, Sebastian," she said with giddiness. "And you?"

"I'm quite well, Miss Ashby."

"I'm so glad to hear that."

It wasn't easy wooing the viscount, she thought with ire. A deuced bother, really. Henrietta wasn't a soul to practice patience. She didn't have much restraint when it come to her temper, either. Worst of all, though, was her inability to flirt with aplomb. She could never find her voice when in the viscount's presence. Her emotions overwhelmed her and her mouth grew dry until she squeaked like a mouse.

"You look lovely this evening, Miss Ashby."

"Thank you, Sebastian."

His smoldering blue gaze dropped to caress the swell of her bosom.

It's working, she thought. *He's finally going to see me as a woman!*

He then whispered, "I think your gown is too scandalous, Miss Ashby."

She blinked, bemused. "What?"

"I suggest you run back to your room and fetch a chemisette."

And with that, he bowed and walked away.

Henrietta remained in the entranceway, dumbfounded. A chemisette! She had draped her body in the softest of silk—and all but exposed her bosom with the low cut of her neckline—and he told her to cover up!

She was going to wring his neck!

Henrietta glared at Ravenswood as he approached Papa and engaged in conversation with the baron. She bunched her fists ... And then tears welled in her eyes.

"Oh, hell's bells."

Henrietta removed her mask and dashed across the ballroom with such haste, she bumped into some of the guests. She didn't offer any apologies, though. She just skirted toward the terrace doors, desperate for air.

In the garden, Henrietta searched for a private nook and soon settled on a stone bench. She waved her mask to cool her flushed cheeks, now stained with tears.

The insufferable rogue! Why couldn't she have set her cap for a more amiable gentleman?

Because only Ravenswood makes your heart pinch in expectation of a touch … a kiss.

She sighed. It was true. Only Ravenswood disturbed her dreams and ruffled her temper and made her want to do the most inappropriate things to capture his attention.

And yet, everything she had done to make an impression on the scoundrel had failed. What was she going to do to get the viscount to admit his true feelings for her?

Henrietta heard a soft groan. She spotted a couple in the moonlight, a short distance away, engaged in the most passionate kiss—and her heart throbbed with longing at the sight.

"I'd give my baby toe to be kissed like that," she whispered.

The couple soon flitted off.

Henrietta sighed. She pressed her lips together, deep in thought. It was clear she needed help charming Ravenswood. A teacher of some sort. But who could she ask for assistance? Her sisters?

Henrietta mulled that over for a bit, then decided against the idea. She might have four elder sisters, all married, but her kinfolk were too prim and proper to offer advice on attracting a mate.

Where could Henrietta go to learn the art of seduction?

"Drat!" she muttered.

Just then a falling star sailed across the midnight sky, and it must have dropped an idea into her head, for she gasped, a wicked thought coming to mind.

The gossip sheets! That's it!

She remembered the infamous story now; she had read all about it over her morning tea.

Henrietta was filled with hope again. She dried her tears. And she smirked with satisfaction.

I'm going to show you scandalous, Sebastian.

~ * ~

Sebastian Galbraith, Viscount Ravenswood, eyed the hoyden bounding across the dance floor, stumbling into guests without so much as a "beg your pardon." The chit was determined to ruin herself, wasn't she? Didn't she care about her respectability? Didn't anyone else?

"Leather tips!" The baron beamed. "Can you believe it, Ravenswood? Leather tips at the end of cue sticks. Why, it's ingenious. It will revolutionize the game of billiards, I dare say."

No, it looked like no one else was sensible to Henrietta's antics, least of all the doting Baron Ashby. It seemed the task to admonish the minx would have to fall upon Sebastian.

Well, she was akin to a sister. Perhaps he should do his "brotherly" duty and scold the chit? No one else was going to discipline her, it seemed. Besides, he didn't want the girl to end up a spinster, pining over him while discouraging every other eligible bachelor with her wild behavior. It just wasn't right.

Sebastian turned toward the baron. "Will you excuse me, my lord?"

"Quite. Quite." And without missing a syllable, the baron fixed his gaze on the unsuspecting gentleman to his other side, and resumed his narrative on the innovation in billiards.

Sebastian crossed the ballroom and slipped into the garden, searching for the elusive Miss Ashby. He soon found her familiar figure on a bench—gazing at a groping couple in awe.

Why, the naughty little vixen. He'd never pegged Henrietta for a voyeur. And when he heard her pining voice—"I'd give my baby toe to be kissed like that"—he couldn't help but smile.

He removed his mask. "Miss Ashby?"

She jumped to her feet.

"I didn't mean to startle you," he said. "Forgive me."

"What are doing here, Sebastian?"

"I must speak with you."

"About?"

"About etiquette. You must bridle your outrageous behavior."

"I beg your pardon?"

"I am part of this family, Miss Ashby. If you cause a scandal, it reflects poorly upon all of us."

She snorted. "What scandal?"

"Really, Miss Ashby? How about darting across the ballroom like your skirt was on fire? And jostling guests?"

"It won't make the *Times*."

He frowned. "Why did you run off in such haste?"

"I needed air, is all." She fastened her mask again. "If you will excuse me, Sebastian. I must meet Mama in the ballroom."

"Not yet, Miss Ashby."

He'd hoped the darker timbre of his voice would instill in her the significance of the matter, but it only made her lashes flutter.

He sighed. When was the minx going to give up her childhood fancy for him? He was stumped. He never touched the girl. He always called her Miss Ashby. Frankly, he played the part of the utter dud. One would think she'd have lost interest in him by now.

"I lied, Miss Ashby."

"About what?"

"I'm not concerned with the family's reputation, but yours."

She thrust her bosom toward him. "Really, Sebastian?"

He wanted to laugh. Her adorable attempts at seduction amused him. If it wasn't in the chit's best interest to marry a respectable bloke, he'd keep her around as a quaint diversion. "Miss Ashby, you must find yourself a proper husband."

A curt bob of the head. "I absolutely agree with you."

Not me, he wanted to clarify, but said instead, "And if you continue in this brash manner, you'll be ruined."

"Yes, ruin me."

He quirked a brow. "What?"

"I mean, I will not be ruined." She blinked a few times. "You exaggerate, Sebastian. I really must return to the ballroom now."

She lifted her gloved hand to push him out of the way, but before her fingers brushed his arm, he stepped off the garden path, allowing her passage.

Was that a whimper of disappointment he heard?

Sebastian let out a frustrated sigh. He wasn't the only bachelor in Town, didn't she know? Why set her cap for him, and not some other, more agreeable gentleman? Why the stubborn refusal to give up on him?

He had to get away from the girl, take a sojourn. Stay out of the incorrigible chit's sight for a few months. The Continent would do him good, he thought. Give him an opportunity to have a bit of sport. Henrietta might find herself another mate in the meantime.

He could hope.

CHAPTER 2

"Are you sure this is a good idea, Miss Ashby?" said her maid.

"I'm sure, Jenny."

Well, Henrietta was almost sure it was a good idea. She tried to convince herself this really was the best—the only—choice she had to make Ravenswood her husband. If she even said the word husband, Sebastian blanched. If she tried to touch him, he recoiled. If she bared her bosom, he rebuked her for it. One would think the man had no regard for her.

But Henrietta knew that wasn't true. She thought back to a time, about two years ago, when the whole family had gathered for her niece's christening. Henrietta had been late for the ceremony, and while rushing to join the family, she'd knocked over her mother's cherished vase. She was sure to get the strap from Mama—Papa never disciplined her—but then Ravenswood had come along and accepted the blame for the mishap, saving her hide. He had been so gallant. He had cared for her then. And he cared for her now. Why wouldn't he just admit it?

She sighed. She didn't know why the viscount was being so stubborn. She didn't know much about men, in truth. And that's why she was travelling down a country road in the dead of night. She needed to take drastic measures to make Ravenswood hers.

The carriage turned a bend, and there, nestled amid the trees, was a grand house: a castle really, with its spire roof tops and stone façade. It was reminiscent of the royal chateaux she'd seen in French paintings, classic in presentation and design, with rows of tall glass windows, all reflecting a brilliant glow of candlelight.

"It's beautiful," she breathed.

As the carriage rolled to a halt, her admiration turned to reservation, and she bunched her skirt in unease.

Don't panic!

She had done everything to preserve her reputation. She had brought along a chaperone. She'd hired a hackney to transport her to the country. She'd even dressed in plain clothes and covered her head in a hooded cloak to conceal her identity.

What could possibly go wrong?

Three male servants emerged from the house, each young and handsome—and very attentive. One opened the carriage door, one produced a stepping stool, and one offered his gloved hand in gentlemanly support.

A hesitant Henrietta stepped out of the carriage, accepted the offered hand, pressed her slippered foot into the cushioned ottoman, and marveled at the well-orchestrated attendants.

She had to admit, this wasn't the sort of reception she'd expected from Madam Jacqueline, so warm and inviting. According to the gossip sheets the woman was a reclusive curmudgeon, grieved by the loss of her charm and beauty. Henrietta was delighted to learn it was all a fabrication. She'd dreaded meeting such a notorious woman. Now their rendezvous might even be agreeable.

Jenny stepped out of the carriage next before the door was closed, the foot stool confiscated, and a sweeping gesture made toward the entrance.

"This way, mademoiselles," said a footman.

Henrietta skirted inside the house, her maid right behind her.

"Will you allow me to take your cape?" asked a servant.

Henrietta pinched the stays, unnerved.

"You are safe here, mademoiselle," he assured her.

After a few anxious moments, Henrietta loosened her grip on the stays, and the cloak was whisked away.

It was then her eyes beheld the true majesty around her. She had been to many balls in many prestigious homes. She had attended court and dined in country splendor. But she had yet to encounter the likes of a Scandinavian ice palace in the heart of English society. Why, it was a scene from a northern fairy tale. A Valhalla, of sorts, fit for a Viking god or warrior.

How delightful!

A footman stepped forward and extended his arm. "If you please, mademoiselle."

The two remaining servants circled Jenny, hindering her attempt to follow.

"Madam Jacqueline wishes to see you alone," said the footman. "Your maid will be well looked after, I assure you."

A wary Henrietta nodded. She then smiled at a nervous-looking Jenny, vowing, "I'll be back soon."

Henrietta was escorted through the ice palace to a nearby salon. As soon as she entered the room, she was dazzled by the turnaround of décor. She had departed the pleasures of Scandinavia and had traveled thousands of miles east to the mystic Orient.

The footman gestured to a red divan. "Mademoiselle."

Henrietta settled against the rich cushions. A small fire crackled in the hearth; the smoldering warmth deflected by an embroidered Japanese screen.

"Sherry, mademoiselle?"

She received a silver goblet, shaped like a tiger's head. "Thank you."

The footman bowed and quietly vacated the room.

What had she gotten herself into? thought Henrietta. The more time she spent in the peculiar wonderland, the more she wondered if perhaps she'd made a dreadful mistake, after all.

And then she remembered the disastrous masquerade. After all the guests had departed, Sebastian had made a ghastly announcement:

"I'm off, Miss Ashby."

"Goodnight Sebastian," she'd murmured, mounting the stairs.

"I'll see you at Christmas."

Christmas!

She'd whirled around. "What do you mean Christmas?"

"I've decided to take a trip, Miss Ashby."

"Where?"

"Truthfully, I've no idea. But I'll be gone for six months. Take care, sister."

And with that, he'd made a curt bow and sauntered away, leaving Henrietta on the steps, mouth agape.

It was then she'd realized, however scandalous her intentions, she *had* to go through with her plan. Soon Sebastian would see her but once a year. And then not a'tall. Soon he'd be lost to her forever.

Henrietta stifled a gasp when the wall gave way—well, a paneled door in the wall—and a figure emerged from the nook.

A rather small figure.

The woman, draped in a caftan and a turquoise turban to match, wasn't more than three score and five years—and not very pretty at that.

Aye, the years had marked her features. But what about the hard slant of her jaw? The wide breadth of her nose? Henrietta wonder, with such attributes, if she had ever been pretty, even in youth. Her eyes were unique, though, a most unnatural shade of mist green. A very captivating pair. But still, *she* was London's most renowned courtesan?

Henrietta furrowed her brow. "Madam Jacqueline?"

The small woman settled on a divan opposite Henrietta, her jewels winking in the candlelight. "As you see."

Henrietta sipped the sherry, throat parched. "Thank you for agreeing to meet with me."

"I must admit, I was surprised to receive your letter."

Not nearly as surprised as Henrietta was to greet the notorious courtesan. According to the gossip sheets, Madam Jacqueline had so enamored a Russian prince, he'd all but made her his royal bride, to the outrage and near revolt of St. Petersburg. She had charmed a French duke so terribly, he'd put a pistol to his head when she'd broken off their affair. And then there was the tale of the ruined Italian noble, so bewitched by Madam Jacqueline that he'd surrendered his entire fortune to her. Or so the stories had claimed. And Henrietta was most curious to know if these stories had been fabricated, too.

"It is all true, Miss Ashby."

Henrietta yelped and placed her fingers over her mouth. Heavens, had she sputtered her thoughts *aloud*?

No. Wait. She had done no such thing. Then how …?

"You are a witch?" she said, disquieted.

The woman laughed, a deep and husky sound, oddly soothing to the ear. "Some might think so, but I assure you, I do not dabble in the black arts."

"But you read minds."

"Nonsense, child. I read faces. And you are thinking: *How can this small, plain and extravagant woman be the famous Madam Jacqueline?*"

Henrietta didn't confirm the woman's observation; she felt that rather rude. Instead, she said, "I need your help, Madam Jacqueline."

"Yes, you mentioned that in your letter. Do go on."

Henrietta blushed.

Oh, out with it, silly. It's why you're here!

"Well, you see, I need to learn how to ..."

"Seduce a man?" said Madam Jacqueline.

"Yes!"

Henrietta sighed. With Madam Jacqueline's talent for observation, Henrietta might not have to voice her bashful thoughts too often. What a boon!

The woman cocked her head. "Do you know what I am, Miss Ashby?"

Henrietta nodded, thinking: *It's why I've come to see you!*

"And what am I?" asked the woman.

"Well, you're a ..."

Henrietta pondered the answer. Was "courtesan" the proper word? Or would the woman be offended by the term? Henrietta couldn't imagine so, but still, she really needed Madam Jacqueline's help, and she didn't want to say anything that might upset—

"I am a philosopher, Miss Ashby."

Henrietta blinked. "Pardon?"

"A philosopher," she repeated. "I entertain men of great wealth and power; they visit me to ask my advice. I inspire men, Miss Ashby, where their wives have failed."

"Oh," said Henrietta. She hadn't considered Madam Jacqueline in *that* kind of light.

"And who do you wish to inspire, Miss Ashby?"

Henrietta's heart throbbed. "Sebastian."

"And how do you intend to inspire Sebastian?"

"I'm not really sure," she admitted.

"Hmm." The woman cast her a critical eye. "Do you intend to bat your pretty lashes at him until he falls at your feet? You will never win his heart like that, Miss Ashby."

After so many years of frustration and anguish, Henrietta pleaded, "Then *how* will I win his heart?"

"You must be his friend and his lover."

Henrietta slumped her shoulders. She didn't understand the first thing about being a lover. She couldn't even get Sebastian to kiss her! And friendship? After four years the man still treated her like a child. How would they ever become friends?

"I don't know how to be either," she whispered, crestfallen.

"There are ways to learn."

Henrietta's eyes brightened. "Does this mean you'll help me?"

The woman perused her for a thoughtful moment. "I will."

"Oh, thank you, Madam Jacqueline!"

The woman reached for a leather-bound book on a small table next to the divan. She opened the tome to a random page and set it before Henrietta. "To begin, tell me about the couple in the picture."

Henrietta leaned forward, balked, then slammed the book closed.

Mercy, did lovers actually do *that*?

Madam Jacqueline quirked a painted brow. "You will start by going through the entire book, Miss Ashby. You will stare at every page, and stare and stare again, until you can look at the pictures without blushing ... until you want to engage in those very acts with Sebastian."

Could she really do such a thing?

But one look into Madam Jacqueline's wise and charismatic gaze, and she understood she didn't have a choice. If she wanted to seduce Sebastian, she had to learn to be both his friend *and* his lover.

"I'll do as you say, Madam Jacqueline. And I'll pay you for your teaching."

If I survive the lessons. What a mortification this was going to be!

"I have no need of your money, Miss Ashby."

"Then why are you doing this?"

The woman smiled, a very charming gesture. “I wish to pass along my wisdom. I feel it a terrible thing to waste.”

CHAPTER 3

The manor house, nestled amid snowy mounds, stood prominent against the winter land. Smoke curled from each of the six chimneys, and in the fading afternoon light, the candle flames, sparkling from each of the glazed windows, gave the home a warm and inviting glow.

Sebastian reflected upon the quaint country dwelling—and the quirky family that hibernated within its walls. Six months ago he had quit England for the Continent. It'd been an agreeable trip, filled with gluttony and sinful pleasures. But all good things must come to an end. Six months ago he had severed all communication with the Ashby family, hoping the youngest and most willful of the brood, Miss Henrietta Ashby, would set her cap for a more deserving gentleman. Now he'd returned to see how his plan had fared.

The sleigh slid to a stop, the sleigh bells chiming, announcing Sebastian's arrival. He was wrapped in bear skin to keep warm and tossed aside the fur, stepping out of the cutter.

The butler greeted him at the door and helped him divest his greatcoat, while a footman fetched his luggage.

"Ravenswood, my good man! How delightful to see again!"

Sebastian turned toward the short and rotund baron, shuffling toward him, arms outstretched.

He extended his hand in greeting. "Thank you for the invitation, Lord Ashby."

"Nonsense, my boy, you're family. Family, I say. The Yule festivities would not be the same without you."

He nodded in appreciation. "How are you, my lord?"

"Oh, the same, Ravenswood. The same. A few pounds heavier, a few white hairs shorter."

The viscount smiled. For all the baron's foolery, he was a charming old fellow. "I'm glad to hear it, my lord."

"We've missed you these last six months. Come. Join me for a drink."

Sebastian cocked his head in acquiescence.

The baron beamed.

As Sebastian trailed his host, he sensed something was amiss. He glanced around the house, inspecting the furniture, the artwork, the mirrors; all were in the right position, just as he remembered.

What was it then?

"The hounds."

The baron looked over his shoulder. "I beg your pardon, Ravenswood?"

"Where are the hounds, my lord?"

"In the kennel, I'm afraid. Lady Ashby ordered the poor boys out of the house after one, er, decorated her favorite rug. The boys are not permitted inside the house for the rest of the day. Punishment, you know."

Ah, so that's what was wrong. No hounds. Sebastian knew there was something missing underfoot ... No. Wait. That wasn't it, either.

He followed the baron into the study and settled in an armchair, wondering: what was the nameless anomaly that nagged him?

The baron made his way over to the cabinet and collected a decanter, filling two glasses with a splash of brandy.

"How was the Continent, Ravenswood? Drab compared to our mighty England?"

It was nothing of the sort, but the viscount wasn't about to admit that. He accepted the drink and offered a toast: "To England, my lord."

"Here. Here."

The baron took the opposite armchair and plunked his feet on the ottoman with a sigh.

Sebastian glanced around the study. *What* was that strange sensation? He examined the bookcases, the desk, then stared at the door as if waiting for … a little hoyden.

That's it! That's what was missing. Henrietta.

Where was Henrietta?

She was always the first person to greet him. For the past four years, without fail, she'd bounded up to him in salutation before he'd set both boots inside the house. It was the only time she was ever *on* time for anything.

"I say, Baron, is the whole family here?"

"Quite. Quite. You are the last of the guests to arrive. So good of you to join us, Ravenswood."

Sebastian still stared at the door, waiting for it to open, anticipating the chit would come fluttering into the room, out of breath and professing apologies for being late in her welcome.

She did nothing of the kind.

Sebastian frowned. "Is the family well, Lord Ashby?"

"In capital health, my dear boy."

Odd. If Henrietta wasn't ill and tucked away in bed, then where was she? Perhaps the girl was wed? Now *that* was an agreeable thought.

"And how fares Miss Ashby?" he asked, taking a sip of brandy to warm his belly.

"Henry? Capital. Capital. The darling boy is such a pleasure."

Sebastian grimaced at the "darling boy" bit. If Henrietta had been raised as a proper young miss, she would be married by now, not hounding him.

"I've been gone so long, my lord," said Sebastian. "Has there been any cause for celebration at the house?"

Like a wedding, perhaps?

"Oh, yes!" the baron cried. "A happy event indeed."

Splendid! The girl was married. Sebastian was free of the smitten chit and her scandalous behavior.

"I have leather tip cue sticks!" The baron clapped his hands. "Isn't it grand? We must play a game of billiards, Ravenswood."

Not exactly the good news Sebastian had been hoping to hear.

The viscount tried another tactic. "My lord, about Miss Ashby?"

"Yes, Ravenswood."

"Is the girl fond of anyone?"

"To be sure, Ravenswood. To be sure. The dear boy's fond of many folks. He's got a most generous heart."

Sebastian took another swig of brandy, and since subtle conversation was not the baron's forte, asked outright, "My lord, is the girl engaged?"

"Rot!" cried the baron. "Henry has more sense than to get himself leg-shackled. Nasty business, I say. Drives a poor chap into hiding."

The viscount sighed. "Yes, nasty business."

The baron gave a curt nod. "One needs a strong disposition to be riveted. An authoritative voice. A firm hand. Now I have such a disposition and can weather the storms of matrimony, but dear Henry is a most delicate boy, and I feel better suited to a quiet life at home."

"Quite right, my lord." Sebastian downed the rest of the brandy. "But is the girl, perhaps, interested in a gentleman?"

"Interested? My Henry?" The baron looked at the ceiling. "Why, I don't think so, Ravenswood."

"Are you sure, my lord?"

"Oh, yes, quite sure. Why, I'd hear all about it from Lady Ashby if Henry had a beau. Now back to my cue sticks …"

The viscount turned his thoughts to more pressing matters. The girl was still unattached, was she? He had underestimated her stubbornness. Well, he'd just have to go back to the Continent. Traipse through the Parisian underworld and consort with the Italian demimonde. He *had* to disabuse Miss Ashby of her girlhood fancy for him. He'd no choice, it seemed, but to return abroad—after Christmas, of course. He wasn't a total degenerate. He adhered to some religious observances.

"Please excuse me, my lord," said Sebastian. "I would like to rest before dinner."

"Capital idea, Ravenswood! The butler will show you to your room."

Sebastian headed for the door. "I will see you at dinner, my lord.

"Yes, of course, my good man. At dinner."

And with that, the baron closed his eyes and went to sleep.

Sebastian vacated the study and made his way through the familiar passages. He didn't need the butler to show him to his room. He had occupied the same chamber—whenever he'd visited the family—for the last four years. But a question baffled him. If Henrietta wasn't even engaged, then why hadn't she come down to greet him?

CHAPTER 4

You're leaving after the holidays?"

Sebastian glanced at his flabbergasted brother. "That's right, Peter."

"But you just returned home, Seb. Why run off again?"

Because Sebastian needed to separate from a certain incorrigible hoyden, who happened to be late for dinner—as usual. Not that the family seemed to mind. Accustomed to the girl's tardiness, the brood had simply immersed themselves in the freshly cooked fare, an empty chair left for Henrietta at the far end of the dining table.

Sebastian sliced open the broiled fish. "I have a rather pressing matter of business to attend to on the Continent."

Peter snorted. "You mean you have a pressing itch in your—"

"Peter," Sebastian drawled. "Mind your manners at the dinner table."

Peter shook his head. "I don't understand you, Seb."

"Oh?" He quirked a brow. "And what don't you understand?"

"Why do you have to go abroad to attend to 'business.'?" Peter whispered. "What the deuce is the matter with English wenches?"

Sebastian chuckled. "Nothing a'tall, bother. I just need to go abroad. Trust me."

The other man sighed. "Well, we're here till Twelfth Night, so let's make the best of what time we have together. Did you hear the baron has leather tip cue sticks? We should play a game of billiards."

"I suspect we will, Peter."

Sebastian looked at the other guests. The "we" included the baron and baroness, and *all* the Ashby sisters and their respective spouses. Sebastian didn't really get along with the other gentlemen, though; too prudish for his taste. He only got along with his brother, really. And the baron, of course. Sebastian just wasn't the sort of man to make friends easily or engage in platonic pleasantries. He was more of a flirt. A seducer. And after the death of his parents from consumption almost ten years ago, he'd immersed himself in more unsavory pursuits.

"By and by," said Peter, "why are you here? I'm bound to the family till death, but you've no familial obligation. Unless, of course, you want the last of the sisters for yourse—"

"Finish that thought and I'll stab this fork into your hand."

Peter chuckled, well aware of his brother's plight with Henrietta. "And spatter blood all over Lady Ashby's linen tablecloth? Heaven forbid."

"Then I suggest we let the matter rest."

"Sound advice, but I feel I must warn you, Seb, you might have to settle down one day, however foul the idea."

"Rubbish."

Sebastian was never going to tie the marital noose around his neck. Whyever for?

"The estate needs an heir," said Peter.

"Yours will do just fine."

A sigh from Peter. "While nothing would please Penelope and me more, you know very well it might never come to pass."

It was a rotten truth, and Sebastian knew it. The three other Ashby sisters were already mothers—their brats, thank the heavens, tucked away in the nursery—but Penelope had yet to have a babe, much to the sorrow of both her and her husband.

"The duty might fall upon you yet, Seb."

Bloody hell. Still, Sebastian wouldn't dwell on on the ghastly matter. Penelope was only six-and-twenty, while Sebastian was thirty-two and too jaded to even contemplate marriage. There was still plenty of time for the young woman to produce an heir. He needn't fret about the dreadful responsibility. Not yet anyway.

From across the table, Penelope offered him a warm smile. "Tell us, Ravenswood, has the fashion in Paris changed much since the spring?"

"Oh, yes," he said with a flirtatious wink. "But I admit, I paid little attention to the vogue."

"Lud!" from the other sister, Roselyn. "Why couldn't you have been more of a dandy, Ravenswood, and observed the trends?"

Sebastian bowed his head. "It was dreadful of me, I know."

Next Cordelia chimed, "Did you happen to notice the more fashionable colors, Ravenswood?"

"Pink, I believe."

"Pink?" Tertia, the last of the sisters, wrinkled her brow. "Surely not, Ravenswood. Pink was last season's color. You must be mistaken."

But before Sebastian could offer another opinion, Henrietta appeared.

Sebastian bristled.

The chit paused in the doorway, her head held high, her shoulders set back. A charming smile touched her lips; a playfulness twinkled in her eyes. After a brief delay, she entered the room with uncanny confidence, her rich, auburn locks in a whimsical twist, tendrils bouncing by her ears.

What had happened to the girl?

A few cordial greetings drifted from the table, but otherwise the gathered party made no remark about Henrietta's transformation. Was the family so distracted by hunger? How could they just sit there and not gawk at the hoyden skirting across the room?

Skirting? No, she wasn't skirting. She was swaying. Artfully so. The soft and rhythmic rustle of her petticoats tickled his ears as she swished this way and that. Blimey, the girl had hips!

"Henry, my boy," the baron shouted a jovial salutation. "How good of you to join us."

Henrietta pressed her lips to her father's brow—her round rump arched ever so slightly. "Good evening, Papa."

A peculiar spasm gripped Sebastian's heart. What the deuce was the matter with the girl's voice? It was deep and husky; the inflection steady. Did she have a cold?

Sebastian watched, transfixed, as an attending footman helped Henrietta into her seat. With a flick of the wrist, she unfurled her napkin and set it across her lap. A meal was placed before her, and she set to work on gracefully devouring the fare—without so much as glancing his way.

"Well, Ravenswood?"

Sebastian snapped his attention back to Tertia. What were they talking about again? Paris? Clothes? Colors? That's it! "Blue, I believe."

Peter choked.

Tertia lifted a delicate brow. "I should purchase a blue mare, Ravenswood?"

Sebastian frowned. "We're not talking about the Parisian vogue?"

"No, Ravenswood," said Tertia. "Ponies. For my Edward's fifth birthday. We were talking about the best breeds."

"My apologies, sister."

Sebastian glared at Henrietta again. The girl was huge! Two dress sizes bigger, he was sure. What's more, the precise cut of her red velour frock made sure to highlight those striking curves. And damned if she hadn't sprouted a figure worthy of notice.

"What do you think, Ravenswood?"

Blast it! Not again. What was it this time? Birthdays? No, breeds! "I believe a Shetland is the best choice."

Tertia coughed. "I most certainly will *not* serve horse flesh at my Eddie's birthday dinner!"

Sebastian stifled an oath.

His brother leaned in to whisper, "Whatever is the matter with your ears?"

His ears might be defective, but there was nothing the matter with his eyes. "Look at her, Peter."

"Who?"

"Henrietta, you fool!"

Peter did as he was told. "What about her?"

"Don't you notice something different about the girl?"

Peter furrowed his brow. "No, not really. Then again, you've been gone six months. I'm sure we all seem a bit different to you."

"*You* are tryingly the same, brother." Sebastian glanced at Henrietta, then back at Peter. "Can't you see the change in her?"

Peter peeked down the dining table again. And once more he affirmed, "There's nothing the matter with her."

Sebastian sensed his temples throbbing. "She's twice her normal size!"

Peter choked again. "Good heavens, Seb, are you mad!? She's nothing of the sort."

"Look closely."

"I *have*. She's hardly half a stone plumper."

"Rubbish, the girl is ..." So curvaceous, Sebastian's fingers twitched in a most wicked way. "What about the way she eats?"

"What the deuce is the matter with the way she eats?"

Well, for one, she savored her meal with far too much feeling, slowly licking her lips after each bite. Sebastian's breath hitched at the provocative sight.

"Seb, are you feeling all right?"

Sebastian looked at his brother, confused for the first time in a long time. There was something dreadfully wrong with Henrietta. Why was he the only one who noticed?

CHAPTER 5

A gentle snowfall blanketed the earth. Henrietta stood on the terrace in a fur-trimmed wrap and gazed into the distant night.

She had done it! She had followed Madam Jacqueline's advice, and for the first time ever, Sebastian had really *looked* at her. She was giddy. But she had only passed the first of many tests. Still, she was elated. She had wondered over the past several months if she had the strength and skill to go through with the seduction. And tonight she'd proof of it.

Oh, it had been a wretched wait for Ravenswood to come to the house! She had paced her room, her belly in a knot, her rug threadbare from abuse. And then the sleigh bells had chimed, heralding his arrival—and she had paced some more.

Never show too much affection.

It was one of Madam Jacqueline's cardinal rules, and so, instead of rushing to greet Sebastian at the door, like she had in the past, she'd remained in her room, awaiting the dinner bell. Even then she'd delayed her entrance to the dining room. And it had worked. Splendidly, in fact. She had sensed Sebastian's dark gaze on her the entire time.

"Good evening, Miss Ashby."

Oh, that smoldering male voice! How she'd missed it!

Henrietta gathered her features, her heart pounding, and turned to find the most handsome man in creation sauntering toward her.

She couldn't help but sigh. Inwardly, of course. Madam Jacqueline had instructed her on the art of looking composed even when one didn't feel very collected.

Henrietta smiled and curtsied. "Good evening, my lord."

Sebastian stopped dead in his tracks at the title "my lord." It was another one of Madam Jacqueline's basic rules: *take away the familiar until the man longed for it back*. She would not call him Sebastian again until he implored her to do it.

The moment of shock over, the viscount resumed his advance toward her. Snow crunched softly beneath his booted heels. He came to a stop just short of her arms reach, a light dusting of snow clinging to his hair, his coat. The tiny white puffs even settled on his thick and sooty lashes, and Henrietta found herself quite mesmerized by the charming sight.

"How are you this evening, Miss Ashby?"

Her smiled broadened just a bit. Madam Jacqueline had been right. A rake like Ravenswood would pick up on her sensitive sexual signals. She hadn't believed it true, at first. The man had never noticed her obvious attempts at seduction. How would he ever perceive the obscure ones, she had thought?

But a patient Madam Jacqueline had explained to her the power of a sophisticated courtship. The thrill a man obtained from picking up "the scent" and then partaking in "the hunt," as she'd put it.

Henrietta needn't change her appearance or manner in any wild way, the courtesan had said. Just a tweak here. A reform there. A few extra pounds to give her figure the right curves. A throatier voice to invite salacious daydreams. And a confident stride to attract attention.

It was just enough of a transformation to draw Sebastian's notice without disturbing the peace in the household. After all, she didn't want her parents or sisters to realize what she was doing—only Ravenswood.

"I am well, my lord. I'm just enjoying the winter air. It's so crisp and refreshing, wouldn't you agree?"

"Yes, indeed," he murmured.

He was staring at her. Hard. He was trying to decipher the puzzle she had become with those vivid blue eyes of his. He'd never learn the truth, though. He'd never learn the full extent to which she had gone to capture his heart. If he ever found out, he'd ring her neck.

"How was your trip abroad, my lord?"

"Quite pleasant, Miss Ashby. In fact, I intend to return to the Continent after Twelfth Night."

Her heart shuddered. "Really, my lord? We shall mourn the loss of your company."

He was running off again, was he? She wasn't daft enough to believe his flight had nothing to do with her. Well, she'd just have to seduce the mulish man by Twelfth Night.

"And you, Miss Ashby? How have you been these last six months?"

"Very well, my lord."

It wasn't what one said, but how one said it, according to Madam Jacqueline, that really mattered. And so, Henrietta maintained a low and even voice, even under the viscount's penetrating stare.

"Then you are not ill, Miss Ashby?"

"I am in perfect health, my lord. Why do you ask? Do I look ill?"

He paused, then: "You look different."

"Oh?" She quirked a brow. "In what way?"

"I can't quite put my finger on it, Miss Ashby."

I'm sure you can't, she thought impishly. And she intended to keep him perplexed for the next two weeks. She didn't want him to guess her intentions. He'd dash off before Twelfth Night if he suspected she was flirting with him. And she didn't want to spend another six months brooding at home, while he gallivanted across the Continent.

In a coy voice, she said, "You know me so well, my lord."

"Then something *is* amiss?"

"Alas, I'm afraid so." She whispered, "I have a secret."

"And will you share it with me, Miss Ashby?"

"If you promise to keep it private."

"I promise," he said, "on my honor as a gentleman."

Henrietta peeked from side to side, then admitted, "I'm having an affair."

The steam from his lips disappeared as he stopped breathing. Soon, though, icy clouds appeared once more—through his nose. "I don't think I heard you right, Miss Ashby."

"It's dreadful, I know. I'm heartily ashamed of myself."

His voice was taut. "And with whom are you having an affair?"

"Why, with Cook's pastries, of course."

He blinked. "What?"

"Our cook is a wonder in the kitchen." Henrietta twirled her eyes. "Her pastries are divine. I must admit, I've developed an unhealthy fondness for sugared cakes."

Sebastian didn't say anything for a moment. Instead, he rubbed his lush lips together, deep in thought.

Henrietta, bewitched by the movement of his tempting lips, had to quickly lift her gaze to meet the man's eyes again.

"You are teasing me, Miss Ashby."

The rugged drawl of his voice did wonderful things to Henrietta: delicious shivers that rolled over her in rhythmic waves. How she longed to hear that deep and sultry voice in her ear! To feel his warm breath caress her skin.

She fixed a playful smile to her lips to conceal her fluster. "Of course, I'm teasing you, my lord. What's a little banter between friends?"

And since she'd never teased him a day in four years, she could understand the man's bewilderment.

Sebastian lifted a black brow. "Friends, are we? Pray tell me, Miss Ashby, what will we do as friends?"

"We will do as every other couple engaged in friendship."

"Unfortunately, I do not have many friends, Miss Ashby, so I will need your guidance in this matter."

She counted off her gloved fingers. "We shall share each other's company. Tease one another. And, of course, we'll share our deepest and darkest secrets."

"Like a penchant for pastries?"

She quirked a grin. "Precisely, my lord."

"I see." His heated gaze touched her like a hot iron poker. "Well, since we are friends, Miss Ashby, do you have any other deep and dark secrets you'd like to impart?"

The scoundrel was trying to unsettle her with a piercing stare, make her falter and betray her *real* secret. Well, she had just the counter measure for such a wily move.

Henrietta thought about one of the many wicked images in the courtesan's naughty book of pictures: pictures she had come to memorize, even desire. She imagined a naked couple, their limbs intertwined, their lips in very intimate places. And then she looked at Sebastian's lips. She let her eyes rest on the tempting pair as she delved deep into her fantasy.

After a few salacious moments, she lifted her gaze to meet his sharp stare, and smiled. "No more confessions tonight, Lord Ravenswood." She curtsied. "Pleasant dreams."

Skirting around him, Henrietta all but skipped off the terrace. If she hadn't bowled him over before, she'd bowled him over now. Madam Jacqueline had been right. Again.

Think a naughty thought and it would show in your eyes. Something a true rakehell would never miss.

~ * ~

Sebastian stood on the terrace, staring at the winter wonderland. As the minutes ticked by, he looked more and more like a man of snow. He should really get himself indoors where it was warm. But he did nothing of the sort. In truth, he didn't feel the cold. He didn't feel much of anything—except for a smoldering ember burning deep in his belly.

Had the hoyden just leveled him with a sinfully wicked stare? Sebastian was sure the answer was an unequivocal "no." Henrietta was a whimsical chit, nothing more. Which meant *he* was half-baked.

Bah! He was imagining things. He was tired, is all. A sinfully wicked stare, indeed. He snorted. Henrietta was far too innocent. The chit didn't know the first thing about being wicked ... but there *was* something very different about the girl. Why, she'd actually called him by his title! In *four* years, she'd never called him" my lord."

And what was that nonsense about friendship? Did the girl still want to marry him or not?

Something was amiss. Why had she teased him, for instance? An affair with pastries? Had all that sugar gone to the girl's head? Her sweet tooth explained one anomaly, though. Her plump and curvy figure. Hips! The girl actually had hips! Lush and oh-so-round ...

"Bloody hell," he growled and left the terrace. The cold was seeping into his brain, making him imagine all sorts of absurdities. Still, he doubted a warm fire would put his senses to right. He had a quandary on his hands.

Pleasant dreams? Not tonight. Not for a great many nights. Not until he debunked the mystery of the curious Miss Ashby.

CHAPTER 6

"Good morning, Miss Ashby."

It was about bloody time, she thought. She had been waiting for Sebastian for almost an hour. The rest of the family had had their breakfast and dashed off, but Henrietta was on her third cup of tea and growing irritable.

She gathered her composure, glanced toward Sebastian—and let out a little gasp. Mercy, he was stunning! He leaned against the door frame, his arms folded across his strapping chest. He was decked in regal day wear—tight regal day wear—his muscular physique hard to miss, even beneath his clothes.

Since her lessons with Madam Jacqueline, Henrietta had come to admire the masculine form. And the viscount's figure was worth more intimate study.

"Good morning, my lord," she said, a little flustered. "Tea?"

He took the opposite chair. "Thank you, Miss Ashby."

Henrietta reached for the still steaming teapot. As she poured him the herbal brew, she noticed the drowsy look in his eyes, his disheveled curls, and the oh-so-smoky drawl of his voice.

She quirked a grin. Had the handsome viscount not slumbered well? Had a certain temptress, mayhap, haunted his dreams?

"You're up late this morning, Miss Ashby."

Thanks to you, Sebastian.

"There's just so much to do today, my lord."

"Such as?"

Such as seducing you.

"Well, there's the skating party to organize," she said. "My sisters and I have decided to take the children to the pond for an afternoon of sport."

"Have a jolly time, Miss Ashby."

He then took a bite from a pastry, and Henrietta's thoughts scattered like leaves in the wind. A heat invaded her belly as he savored the biscuit; a most titillating sight. And she soon scratched out the image of the pastry from her mind and put herself in its place. At the thought of Sebastian doing to her what he was doing to that confection, her whole body started to hum.

"Miss Ashby, are you all right?"

He reached for a napkin to wipe his fingers, staring at her the whole time.

Henrietta had to fight hard to find her voice and keep it from squeaking. "I'm quite well, my lord, I assure you." She took a moment to gather her wits, then said, "I do hope you brought along your skates."

"I'm afraid not, Miss Ashby."

She waved a dismissive hand. "No matter. You can borrow Papa's skates. He doesn't use them anymore."

"Thank you for the offer, but I must decline."

"Rubbish! Why else would you visit if not to enjoy the merry company?"

He gave her a dubious look at that. Was she being too forward? Well, she had to get the dratted man to the frozen pond. She was going to employ a new tactic today: scent.

Scent was *the* strongest aphrodisiac, according to Madam Jacqueline. And Henrietta wholly agreed. Why, just being near Sebastian and taking in the spicy scent of Eau de Cologne had always made her woozy.

Anyway, she'd coaxed from her brother-in-law the name of Sebastian's favorite perfume. And it was time to put that knowledge to good use.

"Come, Ravenswood, we are friends," she persuaded him gently. "And friends often skate together."

"Do they now?"

"Most assuredly."

He stared at her for a long while, then said, "With the children?"

"And my sisters and their husbands. Even your brother Peter is joining in the revelry. So you see, you simply must attend."

After another lengthy pause, he finally sighed. "I've not skated in years."

"Fret not, my lord, I'll be there to catch you if you fall."

~ * ~

Sebastian landed on his arse—again.

He'd had enough. Making his way over to one of the fallen logs, he sat on the makeshift bench and unfastened the leather straps from his boots, discarded the skates. Much better, he thought, and stretched his hands toward the fire, burning in a large tin bucket.

As he rubbed his palms together, his eyes wandered over the frozen pond and the crowd of skaters, until he settled his gaze on a minx dragging two wobbling babes beside her.

With one hand latched on to an unsteady niece and another clamped on to a rambunctious nephew, Henrietta steered the novice skaters, encouraging them, her laughter spirited, but kind, when a little rump hit the sheet of ice. And yet, she moved with grace amid the chaos. In her fur trimmed cape and matching gloves, she appeared a winter faerie, dancing over the icy pond.

"What's this?" Peter scaled the embankment. "Have you given up already, brother?"

"I'm afraid so, Peter. I've lost my touch on the ice."

Peter sat down beside him with a snort. "The only time you've ever 'touched' the ice is with your arse."

"Yes, thank you for the reminder."

Peter stretched his hands toward the fire, too. "What are you doing out here, Seb? You've not skated in years."

"Yes, I know, Peter. I was tricked into the excursion—I think."

"Tricked? By whom?"

"A red-headed vixen."

"Henrietta? Be serious, Seb. She's a darling chit, and all, but she's not one for skullduggery."

Sebastian was beginning to wonder about that. "Well, if she didn't trick me, then what the deuce am I doing out here?"

"You know, I've no idea. But then again, you are a bit of a mystery."

"How's that?"

"Well, you're here for one. At the estate, I mean. A scoundrel like yourself cloistered amid the essence of domesticity. It defies reason."

"Can't a scoundrel visit with family?"

"Yes, of course, but *why* would you come to call at this time of year when every Ashby is gathered at the house? It's beyond me."

"Well, then let me solve this mystery for you, brother. I've come to see Henrietta."

Peter brought his frigid fingers to his lips and blew. "Oh?"

"I'd hoped to find the girl wed, even engaged. But regrettably she's still unattached."

"A vexing predicament."

Was that sarcasm Sebastian detected? "It most certainly is vexing. I've spent the last six months in exile, hoping the chit would find herself a mate. All to no avail, I might add. The baron assures me the girl isn't even interested in another bloke."

"So *that's* why you disappeared to the Continent? And that's why you're going back again, isn't it?" Peter chuckled. "My sympathies, Seb. You've a most dire predicament on your hands. What with a beautiful woman chasing you about, and all."

He growled, "You know damn well nothing can come of it."

"Oh, yes, perish the thought that a man your age should retire his wicked ways and settle down with a lovely lady."

Sebastian glared at his brother. "What do you mean, 'a man my age'? I've yet to sprout a white hair."

"Listen, Seb, it's worth thinking about—"

"No! It's not."

Peter sighed. "And why the deuce not?"

Because Sebastian wasn't about to give up his lascivious habits. A deviant did not "retire" his wicked ways. Such behavior was an incorrigible way of life, an addiction in the blood. And he happened to *like* his wicked ways, blast it! A fussy wife was sure to dampen his lusty disposition, spoil his sinful pursuits. And he certainly wasn't going to marry an adorable minx like Henrietta, who didn't even spark a bit of arousal in him. "I won't marry the girl."

"Oh, Seb."

Peter looked across the pond, and Sebastian unwittingly followed his brother's gaze.

The viscount caught sight of Henrietta with the children, waving to him. Something snagged on his heart, but he quickly dismissed the sentiment.

"Leave it alone, Peter. I don't belong with Henrietta."

An hour later, hungry and tired, the skating party quit the ice and headed for the cozy comforts of home.

Sebastian, too, trailed after the crowd, dodging the children's snowballs—and Peter's. He was about to wallop his pestering brother over the head, when he noticed one member of their group was missing.

Henrietta.

Sebastian looked back at the pond and found her skating alone. She twirled on the ice with grace, her cape fluttering in the breeze.

"Will you join me, Ravenswood?"

She skated to the pond's edge, her cheeks flushed, her lips rosy and plump. The exercise agreed with her, it seemed, for even her eyes sparkled like golden syrup.

"I wouldn't be very pleasant company, Miss Ashby."

She let out a husky laugh. "Rot, Ravenswood! Besides, you need the practice."

She winked at him. A playful wink that struck a chord of … arousal in him? Impossible. He could not have these kinds of feelings for the girl. She was a delightful imp. Always had been. She had not changed *that* much in six months. Nor had he, surely.

"Miss Ashby, I think it best if we both return to the house."

"Oh, I'm not ready to retire, my lord. But you go on ahead. Know this, though, you leave a friend vulnerable in the wilderness."

He flicked a brow upward at the wilderness bit. The house was in perfect view of the pond. He did not protest, though. Instead, he sighed and rested his sore rump on the log once more. "Then I suppose the duty falls upon me to guard you, Miss Ashby—from the wilderness, of course."

"I like that." In a haughty air, she admonished, "You'll sit there, on that rugged lump, rather than skate with me? I warn you, Ravenswood, a friend might start to feel slighted."

"I assure you, Miss Ashby, I've no intention of affronting you."

"I'm glad to hear it." She smiled and moved off again, shouting, "Now put on your skates!"

Why, the bossy little chit! When had she sprouted such an officious disposition? Better yet, *why* had she sprouted such an officious disposition? What was the girl up to?

"Would you like me to come ashore and help you with your skates, Ravenswood?"

"That won't be necessary, Miss Ashby," he all but growled, as he set to work on strapping the bothersome skates to his boots once more. Blast it! How had he gotten himself into this mess—again?

Sebastian made his way back on to the ice, his steps unsteady, and quickly found himself surrounded by Henrietta.

"Here," she said. "Take my hand."

And before he could protest, she clasped him by the hand and secured her other palm to his waist.

Sebastian stiffened at the intimate embrace. Never before had the girl touched him in such a way. He'd been so careful in the past to avoid physical contact, not wanting to encourage her misplaced adoration. But now that she had him in her arms, a bewildering warmth heated his blood.

"You and I have never danced before," she said, as she waltzed across the ice with him—leading at that. The impudent chit. "Why is that, Ravenswood?"

Because you've always hounded me for your husband, that's why.

But he fibbed instead. "I'm a poor dancer, Miss Ashby."

"A poor dancer. A poor skater. Poor company. Do you expect me to believe you flourish at nothing?"

"That's right, Miss Ashby."

"Rot! I think you flourish at a great many things, my lord, and I wish you'd share your accomplishments with me. We are friends, after all."

Sebastian glowered at her, not sure what to make of her request. If only he could think straight. But with the girl's fingers caressing his waist, there wasn't much chance of that happening, so he brushed her palm away from his midriff and set it atop his shoulder—where it belonged.

He realized, belatedly, that wasn't a wise move, for now *his* hand would have to go on *her* waist, and damn if her curvaceous figure wasn't burning up his palm.

"Miss Ashby?" he said with firm purpose.

"Yes, my lord."

And that was another thing. What the deuce did she mean by calling him "my lord" and "Ravenswood" at every turn? It'd been a quaint diversion the first night of his return, but now it was a bloody distraction to hear her call him by his title. He had the feeling the girl was funning with him each time she used the appellation.

"Ravenswood?"

He blinked. "What?"

"You had something to say to me, I believe."

That's right, he did. He had a great many things to say to her. *Why aren't you married yet?* for one. And *What the deuce has come over you?* for another. "Is that jasmine I smell?"

"Why, yes, my lord. Do you like it?"

Like it? He could wallow in it. It was his favorite scent. Not that he'd ever told the girl that. It was a coincidence that she was wearing the one fragrance that could make his head spin.

Blast it, that's not what he wanted to talk to her about. "Miss Ashby—"

"Do you realize you've not stumbled once, my lord?"

She was right, he hadn't.

"You're a very good teacher, Miss Ashby."

"Rubbish. You're just not that poor of a skater."

No, he was a very poor skater, which made his balancing act all the more mystifying.

"You've misplaced your confidence in me, Miss Ashby."

She shook her head. "I don't think so."

Sebastian watched the gentle sway of her dark auburn locks. Her curls were tucked beneath a fetching fur cap, a few stray tendrils bouncing as she twirled on the ice.

She really looked like a snow faerie, so whimsical and fearless. Her bright eyes gleamed with laughter and life. And for just a moment, he could see himself in the honey-brown pools.

And the feeling alarmed him.

"It's getting dark," she said, her lashes fluttering. "We should head back to the house."

She broke away from the embrace and skated to the pond's edge, leaving Sebastian feeling unnervingly cold in the center of the ice.

CHAPTER 7

Be careful, Henry!" Penelope cried. "You'll burn your sleeve!"

"Give the boy some room," said the baron, and waved a hand. "Step back everyone. Step back."

Henrietta pursed her lips in concentration. She eyed the floating raisin in the fiery bowl—not an easy task in the darkened room—and licked her fingertips.

The baroness covered her eyes with her fan. "Oh, I can't look!"

Henrietta dunked her hand into the shallow bowl, grabbed the fiery raisin, and popped the brandy-soaked fruit into her mouth, much to the jubilation of the crowd around her.

"Hurrah, Aunt Henry!" the children shouted in unison. "Hail to the Queen of the Snapdragon!"

Henrietta offered her best curtsy. "Why, thank you, my dear lords and ladies."

The baron clapped his hands. "What a good show, my boy!"

"Thank goodness that's over with," said the baroness, batting her fan. "Lights!"

The footmen whisked about the room, lighting candles, tweaking oil lamps, and stoking the dwindling flames in the hearth.

A breathless Henrietta separated from the family and settled in a window seat, resting her warm brow against the chilled glass. It was Christmas Eve. The parlor was a flutter of activity. And she needed a moment of repose. She still had a seduction to orchestrate—and tonight she intended to move the courtship along.

She pinched the cuff of her sleeve, assuring herself the little velvet purse was still there and hadn't drowned in the bowl of brandy. It concealed a gift for Ravenswood. She then peeked at the door. The mistletoe was still in place. The sprigs would come in handy later in the night.

Ravenswood stood across the room, conversing with his brother. Henrietta didn't look directly at the viscount, though. It was another one of Madam Jacqueline's cardinal rules: ignore the man as much as possible. Make *him* come to you.

And it wasn't long before Henrietta's heart throbbed with excitement.

He's coming!

She scrunched her feet beneath her posterior, making room on the window seat for Sebastian, but the viscount didn't sit next to her. He stopped beside the window, instead, his sharp blue eyes scrutinizing her in that familiar lanky stare.

"How are your fingers, Miss Ashby?"

She shuddered at the sound of his low and throaty voice.

"A bit tender, my lord."

He took the seat next to her. "Let me see your hand."

She quelled a shiver. Oh, he loved her all right! He had never made a public—or private— display of affection until now. What a boon!

She offered him her hand. He clasped her palm in a gentle caress. She all but toppled off the window seat. And when he stroked her fingers with tender regard, it wasn't long before the rest of her body heated as well.

"Perhaps you should retire as Queen of the Snapdragon?"

It took her a moment to gather her wayward thoughts. "Perish the thought. The children would never forgive me."

He let go of her hand; let it slip between his strong fingers. "I'll get you a cold compress, Miss Ashby."

"No, wait!"

Sebastian looked back at her. "What is it?"

"Stay, Ravenswood. I have a present for you."

"A present? For me?"

Henrietta removed the pouch from her sleeve and presented him with the gift. "Here."

Sebastian stared at the satchel with obvious confusion. "What is it?"

She thrust her hand forward in encouragement. "Open it."

He accepted the black velvet purse. For a moment, he did nothing but hold it. Soon, though, he stretched the cords and opened the little sack.

Sebastian removed the ring and lifted it to the light for a better look. It was a gentleman's ring, crafted from gold, the emblem on the surface a Celtic love knot.

Did he recognize the symbol? She hoped not. She didn't want to frighten him off with an obvious show of her affection. But he didn't look alarmed. In truth, he looked very surprised.

"Do you like it, Ravenswood?"

~ * ~

Yes, he liked it. He liked it very much.

Sebastian slipped the ring over his pinky finger. A perfect fit. "Thank you, Miss Ashby. How thoughtful of you."

He'd never received a gift from a woman. It was usually he who did the gift giving, showering a mistress with jewels to keep her content. But he'd never been the recipient of such a gesture himself.

It was a warm sentiment, to receive a gift, especially if the gift was from a … friend.

"I'm afraid I don't have anything for you, Miss Ashby."

"Rot, Ravenswood! We are friends, you and I. And friends give gifts without expecting anything in return."

He looked into her warm brown eyes, so spirited: such a lovely pair of eyes to match such a lovely soul …

"Come, Aunt Henry," cried the children. "Let's play a game of hoodman blind!"

Henrietta flashed him a dazzling smile before she took off with the children. She fastened the blindfold over her eyes and hunched to tickle and tag the children skipping around her.

Sebastian watched her for a time. She was wearing a red velour dress again; the color complimented her dark copper locks, yet contrasted with her creamy complexion. He lifted his eyes to the patch of flesh at her bust … her neck. He pictured his lips tasting the tender skin, his tongue licking the sweet scent of jasmine at her throat …

He slew the salacious thought at once. He was a villain. A jaded wastrel. It was just like him to think such a wicked thought; to corrupt the innocent Miss Ashby in his head.

If only the chit didn't have such a devastating figure: curves in all the right places. He could resist the allure of her smoky voice then, the soft touch of her faerie fingers …

"You look smitten," said Peter."

Sebastian snarled, "Rubbish!"

Peter occupied the abandoned seat next to him. "You have a dreamy look in your eyes, brother."

"I'm just tired."

"A sort of hazy expression across your face," resumed Peter, unperturbed. "I've never seen you like this, Seb."

"There's nothing the matter with me."

"Did I say there was anything wrong with you? Having feelings for a woman isn't a malady, like some might suggest."

Sebastian growled, "I'm *not* smitten with Henrietta."

"Then what do you feel for the girl?"

"Brotherly regard."

"And?"

"And what?"

"Well, I hate to tell you this, Seb, but most men don't look at their sister like she's something tasty to eat."

Sebastian resisted the impulse to crush his brother's throat. "Henrietta and I are just friends."

"*Friends?* Are you mad?!"

Sebastian glared at his brother. "And why not?"

"You can't be friends with a beautiful woman. Hell, you can't be friends with a plain woman! There's just something about you, Seb. You have a tendency to rut about with anything in a skirt."

And since Sebastian *was* having such a difficult time stifling his wicked thoughts about Henrietta, he wanted to throttle his brother all the more for pointing out the wretched truth.

"You're wrong, Peter," he insisted. "I *can* be friends with Henrietta."

He was sure of it.

Really.

CHAPTER 8

Later that night, Sebastian strolled through the quiet house. He fiddled with the ring on his finger, twirling it round and round, thinking of Henrietta.

Six months ago, he had abandoned the chit, hoping she'd find herself a mate. Well, she'd not set her cap for another bloke, but she'd also not pestered him with adoring looks. Instead, she'd offered him friendship.

Sebastian twisted his lips. He didn't have many friends. He had many partners in debauchery, but none he'd consider friends. He didn't know what to make of his newfound "friendship" with Henrietta.

And where had the idea of friendship come from anyway? Six months ago, she'd wanted to make him her husband. Now she just wanted his friendship? Had she given up on the idea of becoming the next Viscountess Ravenswood? Or was the mischievous chit up to something?

He'd no idea. And he couldn't ask Henrietta. She'd only fib if it was a ploy of some kind. One thing was for certain, though. A friend was not supposed to stir the heat in your belly. Peter had been right about that.

Sebastian turned a corner, passing through an arched entranceway—and smacked right into Henrietta.

"Forgive me, Miss Ashby," he said, alarmed.

"Oh, bother that." She rubbed her nose in the most delightful way. "It was an accident. Think nothing of it, Ravenswood."

"Did I hurt you?"

She wrinkled her nose. "Not a'tall."

He cut her a dubious stare. That fragile feminine face crashing into his brutish chest had to sting, even a little. "You've not broken it, have you?"

"Rot!" She sniffed. "I'm stronger than I look."

He had to admire her spirit. Most women would be reduced to tears. Some might even demand reparation: a diamond necklace, for instance. But not Henrietta. He suspected she wouldn't carp even if he'd injured her. And that only made her character all the more mystifying.

"Where were you off to in such haste, Miss Ashby?"

"I was looking for ..."

"For?"

She looked straight at him. "I was looking for my sisters."

He quirked a brow. "It's after midnight. Your sisters are likely in bed. Which is where you should be, Miss Ashby"

"You're quite right." She waved a dismissive hand. "I'll speak with my sisters in the morning. Goodnight, Ravenswood."

"Goodnight, Miss Ashby."

She turned to leave, then paused. "Oh, dear."

"What is it?"

She looked back at him, a blush dusting her cheeks. "I'm afraid we're in a terrible fix."

Was the girl about to faint? Had she bumped into him a little harder than he'd thought?

Sebastian reached for her elbow. "Miss Ashby, are you unwell?"

"I'm quite well, but ..."

Her lashes flitted upward.

Sebastian followed her gaze—and his heart shuddered at the sight of the mistletoe.

Now where had *that* come from? Prior to the Yule festivities, he'd made considerable effort to locate all the ghastly foliage in the house so he could avoid it. And that mistletoe had *not* been there earlier in the evening.

"My lord, I do believe I owe you a kiss."

Blood throbbed in his veins at the sound of her silky-smooth voice. And when she started to chew on her bottom lip in that wanton fashion, blood pounded in other less savory places, too.

She could *not* kiss him. He was adamant. For four years, he'd stood fast to escape the girl's kisses. He would not flounder now; give her reason to believe he cared for her in an un-brotherly fashion. It would only break her heart to learn the truth. He was determined not to devastate her.

"But you and I are friends," she said next, eyes slanted in innocence. "And it wouldn't do a'tall if I kissed you on the lips."

Thank heavens the girl had good sense! *He,* degenerate that he was, hadn't the fortitude to resist such a pair of plump pink lips: lips sprinkled with the scent of jasmine.

"Instead, Ravenswood, I will kiss you where you've never been kissed before."

His breath hitched.

So much for the girl's good sense.

It could not be stopped, the fire burning in his belly at her wanton proposal. The rogue within him took an instant liking to the proposition, the more reasonable part of him tossed to the wayside.

Sebastian could do naught but stare, mesmerized, as she reached for his hand.

He bristled, grasping for his wits, about to pull away, when a jarring voice inside him cried: *Let her show you where you've never been kissed before!*

And after that blasted reproof, he tossed all thoughts of propriety aside.

Henrietta lifted his hand to her lips. Slowly she pulled on the cuff of his sleeve, the fabric skimming his wrist, making him shudder.

A twinkle in her eye, she whispered, "I shall kiss you right … here."

Sebastian closed his eyes, the rogue within him groaning in feral satisfaction, as her warm lips kissed his wrist. The rhythmic movement of her mouth reminded him of other sensual pleasures, too.

"Henry," he breathed, trembling.

It was an entreaty, her name. A plea to break away from him, for he'd not the power to do it himself. And unless the girl abandoned him this instant, she was going to find herself up against the wall—

Sebastian was startled by the sudden surcease. His body still throbbed with repressed ecstasy. And he struggled to regain control of his mind, his very soul.

"There now," she whispered, eyes smoldering with sensuality. "We've not broken with tradition." She smiled. "Goodnight, Ravenswood."

She sauntered into the darkened passageway, leaving him stranded under the mistletoe in abject chaos, for not only had *he* broken with tradition by allowing the girl to kiss him, but he'd done the one thing he'd vowed never to do: call her by her nickname.

CHAPTER 9

Henrietta burst into her bedchamber. She shut the door and sprinted toward the bed, then buried her face in her pillow and let out a squeal of delight.

He had called her Henry! It was the sweetest sound she had ever heard, and every fine hair on her body had spiked to shivering attention.

And she had kissed him! Not on the lips, but still, she had tasted the musk of his skin for the first time—and was utterly intoxicated.

She needed to be bolder, though, if she wanted to seduce the viscount. She had worked on her friendship with Sebastian, but now she needed to nurture the other part of their relationship, too, and become his lover.

Henrietta sat up in bed and reached under her pillow, retrieving a leather-bound tome: a parting gift from Madam Jacqueline.

She opened the book of naughty pictures and traced her fingers over the intimate illustrations, daydreaming about Sebastian.

She had come to admire the sensual pictures in the book; she didn't blush to look at them anymore. Instead, she longed to be with Sebastian—just like the passionate couples in the pictures. Oh, when would she be with the man she loved!

The door suddenly opened.

Henrietta gasped and slammed the tome closed, shoving it back under her pillow.

She stared at the entourage pouring into her room: four sisters draped in wooly wrappers and curling ribbons in their hair.

The women quickly circled the bed like a swarm of angry bees.

Penelope, the eldest of the bunch, placed her hands on her hips, and demanded, "Henry, are you having an affair with Ravenswood?"

Henrietta struggled to gather her wits and slow her erratic heartbeats. Heavens, was she having a nightmare?

"Out with it, Henry," said Roselyn. "Don't idle in bed."

"Speak up, Henry," from Tertia.

"Yes, Henry, do tell us the truth," insisted Cordelia.

Henrietta wanted to plug her ears with her fingers. How had her sisters even noticed the subtle courtship? She had been so careful, acting aloof in public and bolder in private.

"Why do you think I'm having an affair with Ravenswood?" said Henrietta, baffled.

Penelope narrowed her dark brown eyes. "I've just had a little chat with my husband. Peter believes Ravenswood is enamored with you."

Henrietta had a profound urge to hop up and down on the bed. She stifled the impulse and said instead, "Really?"

A snort from Penelope. "My fool husband thinks it absolutely marvelous that the two of you get married."

So did Henrietta. So why didn't her sisters agree?

"I don't understand," said Henrietta. "Why do you dislike Ravenswood?"

"We do like him." Roselyn folded her arms across her chest in an imperious manner. "But we like him as Penelope's brother-in-law, not your husband."

"And why would you *dis*like him as my husband?"

Tertia sighed. "Oh, listen to the dotty girl."

"Henry," said Penelope in reproach, "you must see how inappropriate such a match would be."

Inappropriate? That she marries a respectable viscount? The man that she loved? Was her sister mad?

"I most certainly do not see why it's inappropriate," said Henrietta.

"The poor dear." Cordelia tsked. "She's lost her wits."

"I've done no such thing." Henrietta huffed. "I think *you've* all lost your wits. I've loved Ravenswood for years. Why are you scolding me now?"

"Oh, hush, Henry." Tertia wagged her finger. "You don't really love the man. You're just smitten with him."

Henrietta humphed in indignation.

Roselyn sighed. "Fine, Henry. Then tell us *why* do you love Ravenswood?"

Henrietta could think of a hundred reasons why she loved him; there were so many memories to draw from. The autumn harvest for one. She had been seventeen at the time and very anxious to get her hands on a juicy apple. She'd been about to clamber up a tree to fetch said apple, when Ravenswood had appeared. He'd offered to scale the tree in her stead and had climbed to the tips of the branches to obtain the sweetest fruit for her. Her heart still fluttered at the memory.

"Because," said Henrietta, "he makes my heart—"

"Go pitter patter?" said Tertia.

"Do you get butterflies in your belly?" from Roselyn.

"Or tongue-tied in his company?" said Cordelia.

Henrietta made a moue.

"It's called infatuation, Henry." Penelope folded her arms. "It's not love. Now *are* you having an affair with Ravenswood or not?"

Four piercing stares stabbed her.

Henrietta was stubbornly quiet for a moment, then admitted, "I'm not having an affair with Ravenswood."

Yet!

The sisters released a collective sigh of relief.

"Thank goodness," from Penelope.

"We've come just in time," said Roselyn.

No, you've come at the most importune time, thought Henrietta, and bunched her brow in consternation. "I still don't understand the sudden disapproval of Ravenswood."

"There's nothing sudden about it, m'dear," said Tertia. "Ravenswood was always unsuitable for you. But so long as he didn't return your affection, there was never the danger of a match being made."

"Danger? Unsuitable? What claptrap!" Henrietta clambered to her knees, eyes level with her siters'. "Ravenswood is a viscount. He is most suitable."

"We're not speaking of his title, Henry." Tertia sniffed in displeasure. "We're speaking of character."

"The man is a rogue!" Cordelia blurted out.

Roselyn pinched her. "What Cordelia means is Ravenswood isn't husband material."

"He'll make you unhappy," said Penelope.

Henrietta glared at all four of her sisters. "I know Ravenswood is considered a rogue, but I've every intention of reforming his roguish ways."

Well, not too much, thought Henrietta, for she happened to like a bit of the rogue within him. Ravenswood was ... flirtatious. A reputed rake, he enjoyed the company of a lady. That made him a rogue, true. But the man could make her toes curl. Henrietta quite liked the feeling. And so long as the viscount was faithful to her once they married, he could be as "roguish" as he liked.

"Henry!" Roselyn shook her head. "You can't reform a rogue."

Were her sisters going to use that tired old line: once a rogue, always a rogue? What rot! If *she* could transform from whimsical to wanton, then surely one could go from rake to respectable.

"And you especially can't reform a rogue like Ravenswood," said Tertia.

"Why especially?" Henrietta demanded.

The sisters all looked at one another.

"Ravenswood is handsome, to be sure, and charming," said Penelope, "but he's also sinister."

Henrietta snorted.

"He is," insisted Roselyn. "The talk about him is scandalous. It's frightening, too."

Henrietta furrowed her brow. "What talk?"

"There's talk he's a member of a notorious club." Tertia went on to whisper, "One dedicated to vice."

Henrietta scoffed. "It's just gossip."

The club couldn't be *that* notorious.

It was all just idle talk. The scandal sheets were often wrong about such stuff. Madam Jacqueline had been a purported shrew, yet the woman was nothing of the sort. And while it might be fun to read about gossip, Henrietta wasn't going to choose her mate from the *ton's* society papers! She knew Ravenswood. He was dashing. Wonderful. He was going to make her very happy.

She just had to convince her sisters of that truth.

"No, really," Cordelia chimed, "I've heard the talk, too, Henry. The club is a den of sin, unfit for respectable company."

Henrietta grimaced. "Rubbish!"

"Henry, it's true." Penelope lowered her voice. "Peter often laments about his brother; how he wishes Ravenswood would give up his immoral ways and settle down."

Henrietta thought "immoral" was a tad too strong of a word for a flirt, but she still defended the viscount with a tart:

"Ravenswood *will* give up his 'immoral' ways and settle down." She pointed to her chest. "With me."

Penelope sighed. "Henry, Ravenswood isn't the man for you. You must give up this foolish childhood fancy!"

Henrietta meshed her lips together in defiance. "I intend to follow my heart, sisters."

Four sets of arms went across four sets of bosoms.

"Well, Henry, if your heart is in the *wrong* place, then I suppose the duty falls upon us to protect you."

Henrietta looked at her eldest sister, aghast. "What do you mean?"

But it was Roselyn who enlightened her: "If Ravenswood's got the fool idea into his head that he can have his way with you, then we'll just have to convince him otherwise."

Perish the thought!

"I don't need protecting from Ravenswood," was Henrietta's hasty rebuttal. "He would never hurt me."

"He *will* hurt you, Henry." Cordelia offered her a rueful expression. "You don't know the man a'tall."

"I've known the man for *four* years!"

"No, Henry, you've *dreamed* about the man for four years," said Tertia. "He's not a knight in shining armor."

A lump formed in her throat. Why were her sisters doing this? Petty gossip was no reason to interfere with her life. And so cruelly at that!

Henrietta sniffed. "Why don't you want me to be happy?"

It was a smarting pain, to have her own sisters so determined to quash all her joy.

"That's just it, my dear," said Roselyn in a more soothing voice, "we *do* want you to be happy. And Ravenswood will not make you happy."

Henrietta quelled her sorrow to assert, "*Only* Ravenswood will make me happy. He might show the world his roguish side, but I know his heart. He's not a villain, and I won't listen to any more of this nonsense."

Penelope sighed again. "Willful girl."

"Where does she get it from?" wondered Tertia.

"It's all Papa's doing," quipped Roselyn. "He should have taught her to be a proper lady, to obey her elders."

"Now she'll never listen to reason," said Cordelia.

A nod from Penelope. "Then we'll just have to take care of the matter ourselves."

"No," said Henrietta, panicked.

"We'll make sure Ravenswood stays far away from her," agreed Tertia.

"No!"

"He shan't be allowed to say two words to her," chimed Cordelia.

"No! No! No!"

Roselyn bobbed her head. "It's settled then."

And the four harridans left the room in accord, Henrietta glaring after them, wondering how she was going to get out of this mess.

CHAPTER 10

Henrietta had slept in. She was supposed to spend every waking moment seducing Ravenswood. But last night she'd had the most dreadful dream. It had started out pleasant; her and Sebastian tangled together in an intimate embrace. But just when Sebastian was about to slip his hand beneath her petticoat, four ravens had swooped into the room and pecked out his eyes.

Henrietta let out a huff. Troublesome sisters. What the deuce did they mean by threatening to interfere in her life? Henrietta wasn't a child anymore. She didn't need a guardian—much less *four* guardians. All she needed was a few more rendezvous with Ravenswood.

The dining parlor loomed ahead. Henrietta could hear the chatter. She smoothed her skirt and took in a deep breath before stepping into the crowded room.

Henrietta spotted Ravenswood with ease. There was something about the man: a pull of some sort that always captivated her senses. He looked so dashing, she mused, dressed in a marine blue waistcoat and sapphire jacket. And then there were his eyes. Smoldering. Dark. They fixed on her the moment she entered the room.

"Good morning, Henry!"

The four unanimous greetings had Henrietta seething beneath her composed cheerfulness. She was too late. The harridans had circled Ravenswood at the breakfast table. She couldn't get anywhere near the man.

"Good morning, sisters," she gritted.

She took an empty seat at the far end of the table, and glanced at Ravenswood again. The steel blue of his eyes transfixed her. His stare scorched her. A night apart had not doused the flames of his desire for her. Capital! Now if only she could steal a few moments alone with the viscount to keep that fire burning.

Henrietta inclined her head and smiled. "Good morning, Ravenswood."

But Sebastian had no opportunity to offer a return greeting, for the harridans captured his attention then with a plethora of mindless questions.

"Tell me, what do you think of the French lace at Penelope's sleeve, Ravenswood?"

"How about the exquisite fringe on Cordelia's shawl, Ravenswood? Isn't it grand?"

"Of course, the green ribbon in Tertia's hair is very fetching. Wouldn't you agree, Ravenswood?"

"And let's not forget the chemisette at Roselyn's neck. It's so fashionable, isn't it, Ravenswood?"

Sebastian looked a bit spooked, surrounded by so many demanding females. He hadn't a chance to breathe between answers, never mind look back at Henrietta.

Curse her sisters! They were going to occupy the viscount's every waking moment; create a barrier between her and her love.

Henrietta had a strong urge to flick forks across the table at her sisters.

"Here you are, Henry, my boy." The baron pushed a crumpet across the table. "I saved the last one for you. I know how much you like sweets."

"Thank you, Papa."

Henrietta gave her father a warm smile. She reached for the crumpet and buttered it, all the while telling herself she would not let her sisters spoil the wonderful progress she had made with Ravenswood. She *would* find time to be alone with the viscount. Her sisters could not devastate true love!

Henrietta stuffed the buttered crumpet into her mouth.

"You look weary, sister."

Henrietta glanced sidelong at her brother-in-law, Peter.

"I understand you didn't get much sleep last night." He sighed. "I owe you an apology, Henry, for it was I who spoke with Penelope about Seb's … attachment to you. I didn't think she'd fly into a tizzy about it."

Henrietta swallowed the crumpet, her heart skipping a beat. She didn't have time to be vexed with Peter. She was only curious to know: "Do you really think Sebastian is 'attached' to me?"

Peter looked at her thoughtfully, almost hopefully. "I do."

A surge of emotions stormed her breast.

"Oh, Peter"—eyes darting across the table, Henrietta peeked to make sure no one was eavesdropping—"what am I going to do? My sisters are dead set against my marrying Sebastian."

He whispered, "I'll help you."

"You will?"

Peter nodded. "It's high time my brother marries. You're perfect for him, Henry, and he knows it. He's just being stubborn." Peter paused, then: "You do care for him, Henry, don't you?"

"With all my heart," she said.

"Right then." Another firm nod. "I'll take care of your sisters. You look after Sebastian."

Henrietta would have smothered Peter with grateful kisses if it wasn't for the present company. "Oh, thank you, Peter!"

"Think nothing of it, Henry. This is all my fault anyway. And I intend to fix it." Peter looked down the table at his brother, then said, "I don't know what you've done to him, Henry, but he's not looked so smitten in, well, ever. I'll take care of your sisters, I promise. Oh, and Henry?"

"Yes, Peter?"

"Thank you for caring for him."

She patted his hand. "You don't have to thank me, Peter. The blackguard stole my heart long ago. I didn't really have a choice in the matter."

Peter smiled at that.

"Heavens, look at the time," piped Roselyn. "We'll be late for church!"

The whole table erupted in chaos then.

It was Christmas Day, and the annual Yule service was set to start within the hour.

"Fetch the children!"

"Ready the sleighs!"

Like a herd of horses, the family poured into the passageway and headed for the front door.

Henrietta busied herself getting ready: wrap, muff, fur hat. All the while, she slowly maneuvered herself next to Sebastian. Behind him, really. In the tumult, he didn't notice her standing there.

Henrietta was about to remind him of the kiss they'd shared the other night—when Penelope hooked her arm through the viscount's and pulled him away.

"Come Ravenswood." Penelope smiled. "You'll ride with Peter and me."

Henrietta glared at her sister. She didn't know how Peter was going to get her siblings away from Ravenswood, but Henrietta dearly hoped he'd come up with something soon.

~ * ~

Bless Peter! He'd caused such a ruckus; Henrietta was sure to find a moment alone with Ravenswood.

The whole family was in uproar because Mama's Christmas bell was "missing." It'd been in Mama's family for more than a century, and it was tradition to ring the bell before the Yule feast.

According to lore, the porcelain bell blessed the food and the family, and no one could eat until the trinket had sounded, so the famished family was scouring the house, looking for it.

But Henrietta was looking for something a mite different: Ravenswood.

She bustled through the passageways, peeking into the branching rooms. She noted the parlor was empty, but just then a dark head popped up from behind the settee.

Sebastian.

And he was alone!

Henrietta took a moment to fluff her skirts and ease her thundering heartbeat. With as much aplomb as she could muster, she waltzed into the room.

"Any luck, my lord?"

Sebastian stopped dusting his trousers to stare at her, a seductive glow in his dark blue eyes.

Henrietta was having a hard time keeping her wits about her. For far too long, Sebastian had looked at her with platonic regard. Now each time he glanced her way, a carnal fire burned in his eyes. It delighted her to her very core, his wanton attention, but it also distracted her.

"I'm afraid not, Miss Ashby."

So he was back to calling her Miss Ashby, was he? It didn't matter. She'd have him breathing her nickname again soon enough.

"I can vouch, though, that the Christmas bell is not underneath the settee."

Henrietta busied herself in the room, "searching" for the bell. "Where could it have gone?"

"Perhaps one of the children took it?" he said. "It is a rather shiny trinket, if I remember correctly."

Henrietta peeked inside a vase. "The children pledge on all their toys they did not take the bell." She looked into a tea caddy next. "But with the help of the staff, we should find the bell soon—before we all perish of hunger."

"Miss Ashby?"

She purred, "Yes, Ravenswood."

He bristled.

Drat! She had not meant to sound so wanton.

Coughing into her fingers, she said, "Forgive me. My throat is a bit parched. You were saying, my lord?"

He looked lost for words. In truth, he looked preoccupied with staring at *her*.

Henrietta felt a giddy rush of warm sensations right down to her toes.

"I was going to suggest, Miss Ashby, that you look inside the armoire for the Christmas bell."

"Oh." She skirted to the tall piece of furniture with glass inlays. "What a good idea, my lord."

Henrietta opened one of the glass doors and poked around the shelves.

"You've a parched throat, Miss Ashby?

The fine hairs on the back of her neck spiked as Sebastian approached her. She heard the clicks of his boots and inhaled the scent of Eau de Cologne.

"I hope you didn't catch a chill while you were ice skating," he said.

Confident in Madam Jacqueline's training, Henrietta assured herself she could do this; she could get Ravenswood to kiss her—on the lips this time.

"It's just a little tickle. I'll be fine, Ravenswood."

Shifting through the precious heirlooms in the armoire, she ignored the loud thudding of her heart to ask, "How did you sleep, my lord?"

"Not a wink, I'm afraid."

He was beside her now. Oh, it wasn't fair to her senses, that the man should look, sound, smell so sinfully delicious! It made her attempt at seduction all the more grueling, the distraction he imposed.

"I'm sorry to hear that, my lord."

"Are you really, Miss Ashby?"

"Why, of course, Ravenswood." She peered behind a figurine. "We are friends, you and I. And friends always want what's best for each other."

"Hmm."

His warm breath tickled the soft hairs by her ear, making her shiver.

"About our friendship, Miss Ashby?"

Henrietta stopped searching through the armoire and looked at him. "Yes, Ravenswood?"

A storm raged in his sea-blue eyes. "Do you really think we can be friends?"

The deep rumble of his voice did very pleasant things to her, arousing things. But she stifled her growing passion to reply, "Indeed, Ravenswood. Why do you ask?"

She was careful to match his low tone, to mimic the brewing desire reflecting in his watery gaze.

"It's just that we've known each other for so long, Miss Ashby. I think of you as my—"

"Rubbish, Ravenswood." She moved closer to him, wanting to slay the pestering thought before it took root. She was *not* his sister. She was his soul mate. And she was going to make the dratted man realize it in a matter of seconds. "Our years together will only strengthen our friendship."

"Will they?"

Henrietta tensed. He touched her cheek with the pad of his thumb. Her lashes fluttered under his tender regard.

"They will," she whispered softly. "I promise. Trust me."

His thumb moved to her lips, grazing the swelling flesh in light wisps.

Henrietta could see it in his eyes, his need to taste her. She had a similar longing. It burned and thundered in her veins, the desire to press her mouth to his lush lips.

Her carefully orchestrated seduction was slowly unraveling. She was not supposed to falter under his mesmerizing stare, but the deeper she delved into the glossy pools of his eyes, the heavier she breathed—and the more she thrust her body forward, aching for his touch.

Sebastian lowered his head and breathed, "Henry."

She closed her eyes, heart throbbing, and parted her lips.

"There you are, Ravenswood!"

Reeling, Henrietta smacked her head against the open glass door of the armoire. She clutched her breast in an attempt to quell her rampant heartbeats.

Ravenswood looked no less harried, combing a shaky hand through his curly mane, nostrils flaring.

Penelope and Roselyn flanked the viscount, each hooking a hand—perhaps claw was a better word?—around his arm.

Penelope flashed a dazzling smile. "We've come to escort you to luncheon, Ravenswood."

"The Christmas bell's been found," said Roselyn. "It was hiding in the kitchen, by the fire. One of the hounds must have put it there."

And so Ravenswood was snatched away, like a hapless mortal kidnapped by mischievous faeries.

Henrietta could do naught but stare after him, willing her heart to stay lodged in her breast. Heavens, what a fright! She bloody well had to remember to lock the door next time she tried to kiss Ravenswood.

"Come, Henry!" Penelope sang from the doorway. "Luncheon awaits."

Henrietta scowled at her sister. So close. She had come so close to tasting Sebastian's sweet lips.

Drat!

CHAPTER 11

Sebastian stood beside the window in the library, staring into the stormy night. Insomnia plagued him. He'd not nabbed a wink of sleep since his arrival four days ago. And it was getting to him, the restlessness. He thought of Henrietta more and more. In very ungentlemanly ways.

Snowflakes flicked across the pane of glass, a mesmerizing flurry. He watched the little white dots dance and whirl, trying to banish the image of Henrietta from his mind. But the willful chit refused to go. She pouted her lips at him, so flush, so tempting to taste.

Sebastian moved away from the window. He poured himself another glass of port. Blast it! He was trapped in a mad house. First the peculiar Miss Ashby teased and tantalized his senses. Now her sisters behaved in the most baffling manner, peppering him with idle questions, following him around the house like a litter of puppies.

Sebastian rubbed his brow. Twelfth Night seemed an eon away.

"Forgive me, my lord. I didn't mean to disturb your privacy."

Sebastian bristled. She was dressed for bed in a wooly wrapper. Her billowing russet-red locks glowed in the firelight, hugging the curves of her shoulders, her breasts, her well-rounded hips. She was a bloody temptress, exposing a scandalous patch of bare skin: her toes!

"What are you doing here, Miss Ashby?"

Sebastian was having a deuced hard time purging her from his thoughts without her prancing about in her nightwear.

"I could ask you the same question, my lord."

His fingers burned to trace the shapely outline of her figure, to divest her of that wooly wrapper …

"I couldn't sleep," he said, voice strangled.

"Neither could I." She sashayed to the bookcase and skimmed her fingers over the leather-bound volumes. "I've come to fetch a tome. Some light reading might help put me to sleep."

Staring at her delectable arse was *not* going to put him to sleep, so Sebastian set his port aside and headed for the door. "I will leave you to your reading, Miss Ashby."

She whirled around. "No!"

He quirked a brow. "No?"

"I mean, please don't leave on my account."

He made a curt bow. "Goodnight, Miss Ashby."

"Ravenswood—ouch. Dash it!"

His heart pinched at her cry of distress.

He turned around to find her clutching the back of a chair for support, her expression pained.

He hastened to her side. "Miss Ashby, are you all right?"

"I've stubbed my toe on the chair leg."

"Come here, you foolish girl."

He scooped her in his arms. Blast it! Did she have to feel so damn good in his arms?

He lowered her on the settee. "Let me have a look." He stroked the big toe, swelling slightly. "Can you wiggle it?"

Chewing on her bottom lip, she said, "I think so."

The toe twitched

"It's not broken." He released her foot, for it was causing him an absurd amount of pleasure to touch her in such an intimate place. "Where are your slippers, Miss Ashby?"

"I couldn't find the pair. It was too dark inside my room."

"Of course it was dark." He glanced at the mantle clock. "It's well after midnight. Why didn't you summon your maid?"

She snorted. "And wake the poor girl at this hour?"

"It's the girl's duty, Miss Ashby, to serve you and your whimsical needs. That's why you pay her."

"There's nothing whimsical about my getting a book to read."

"It's very whimsical when you insist on traipsing through the house at such an hour."

She sniffed in defiance.

He glowered at her. "Well, Miss Ashby, after a *sensible*, bare-footed jaunt to the library, how do you intend to return to your room? You can hardly walk."

And *he* wasn't going to carry her. The three steps to the settee he'd taken with Henrietta in his arms had stoked a fire in his belly. He wasn't about to cart the chit through the house.

"Then I shan't go back," she said.

Up went a brow. "Oh?"

"I'll just stay here for the night."

"In the library? Alone?"

"Any why not?"

"I can think of one very good reason."

"Such as?"

"Such as an aghast footman stumbling upon you in the morning. You're half-dressed, Miss Ashby."

"Rubbish." She fluffed her wrapper. "I just need a blanket and I'll be fine."

Sebastian tried not to look at the delicate arch of her ankles and the soft swell of her calves, but the wicked rogue within him was adamant about memorizing the provocative sight.

At last, he blinked and dismissed the vision of her wanton legs. "And I suppose the duty falls upon me to fetch you that blanket? While your maid sleeps soundly away?"

Her lashes fluttered. "Would you mind, my lord?"

He pressed his lips together. The little hoyden always flirted with impropriety. Was she really going to stretch out on the settee in her undergarments? Bloody hell! Of course she was. She was just the kind of rash chit to do such a thing. At least a blanket would cover her dainty toes.

Disgruntled, Sebastian hoisted to his feet. He spotted a coverlet across the room, draped over a chair back, and recovered it.

He returned to the settee.

"Thank you, my lord."

He unfurled the blanket and draped it over her, sorry to see so many delectable curves disappear. No! He was not sorry to see the curves covered. He was grateful to be spared from further temptation. Really, he was.

"You're welcome, Miss Ashby."

She clasped her hands together in her lap. "Will you fetch me a book, Ravenswood?"

"You still want to read?"

"A little, yes."

He sighed and headed for the bookcase. The girl was making him restless. He itched to touch her. To peek under that wooly wrapper …

He was a bloody fool.

He reached the bookcase. "Anything in particular, Miss Ashby?"

"Shakespeare."

His finger paused on a tome. "You read Shakespeare?"

"Voraciously."

He located *Sonnets* and pulled it from the shelf. "Really?"

"You look surprised, Ravenswood."

"I admit, I am, Miss Ashby." He handed her the volume. "It was some time ago, but I remember the family attending a production of *Hamlet* at the theater. And you proclaiming: 'Shakespeare is a dull, old wart.'"

"I'm afraid your memory is a little rusty," she said, a blush dusting her cheeks. "It must have been one of my sisters."

"Perhaps you're right, Miss Ashby. Enjoy your reading. I hope it brings you sweet dreams."

She clasped his hand. "Will you read it to me?"

Sebastian stared at the elfin fingers caressing his palm. Such soft fingers, stirring the heat in his belly with each deliberate caress.

He shuddered.

"Please, Ravenswood." Her forefinger whisked across his knuckles in faerie strokes. "Be a dear friend and read a little to me?"

Thoughts deserted him. He could not come up with an excuse to refuse her request.

How did he keep finding himself in these predicaments?

"Very well, Miss Ashby." He sighed and collected a nearby chair. He took the book from her hand and opened it to a random page. "'My love is as a fever, longing still …'" Sebastian shut the book. "On second thought, I don't think this is a very good idea."

"Rot, Ravenswood!"

"Really, Miss Ashby, I should go." He set the book aside. "It's late."

She placed her hand on his knee this time. "Ravenswood, is something the matter?"

Yes! The wrapper had parted the moment she'd leaned forward, exposing a fluffy night rail—and the plump swell of one breast. His fingers twitched to part the wrapper even more; to mould the lush breast to his hand.

"Well, Ravenswood?"

Henrietta started to rub his knee, exciting the rogue within him.

He gripped her hand with the intent of removing it from his leg, but he squeezed it instead. Not hard. A firm hold to make sure she couldn't pull away. And then he did the most ridiculous thing: he brought her wrist to his lips and kissed it.

CHAPTER 12

Henrietta didn't want to move the seduction along too quickly. It was a risky move, for she might frighten Sebastian away. But with four sisters threatening to devastate all of her plans, she didn't have a choice in the matter. Time alone with Ravenswood was precious, and she needed to make every moment count.

And so she'd used one of Madam Jacqueline's seduction tips: if all else fails, feign injury. A man can never resist rescuing a damsel in distress. In her haste to stop Ravenswood from leaving the library, though, Henrietta really *had* stubbed her toe.

But despite the pain throbbing in her foot, she watched with bated breath as Sebastian lifted her wrist to his lips. And when his warm mouth touched her skin, sending shudders of pure delight throughout her body, she closed her eyes and sighed in total fulfillment.

Sebastian bussed her wrist in feathery wisps, then flicked his tongue over her thumping pulse. He was doing to her what she had done to him the other night. And he was very good at it! Henrietta ached to hold him. But Sebastian was determined to be a tease, pushing up the sleeve of her wrapper, and pressing kiss after kiss to each bare patch of skin.

When he reached the hollow of her elbow, and his dark locks grazed her tender breast, her heart thundered even more, and she stroked his hair, beckoning him closer.

"Ravenswood," she breathed.

He shifted from the chair to the edge of the settee.

A dark fire burned in his eyes. "You're not a little girl anymore, are you, Henry?"

She pushed his hand to her beating heart, the swell of her breast fitting into his palm. "No, I'm not, Ravenswood."

He brushed his thumb across her supple flesh.

What a delicious torment!

"Oh, Ravenswood," she whispered, her nipple puckering under his caress. "Don't stop."

He bussed her throat. "Say my name, Henry."

She gasped when he nipped at her neck, then soothed the bite with the flick of his hot tongue.

Henrietta shivered. "Kiss me."

He lifted his lips to graze hers ever so softly. "That's blackmail, Henry."

"A fair trade," she whispered.

He moved his hand away from her breast. "First, say my name." And he slipped his hand under the blanket and her night rail.

The rogue!

Her knees trembled as he caressed her ankle, her calve.

"Say it, Henry."

Henrietta stared, mesmerized, as his hand roved up her leg, reaching and reaching for—oh, heavens!—the throbbing flesh at her apex.

She cried out.

He nuzzled her cheek. "Say my name, Henry."

He slipped his fingers between the oh-so-sensitive folds of flesh. "Say it, Henry," he beseeched again. "Say my name."

A finger slipped deep inside her wet passage.

"Oh, Sebastian!"

She almost choked on his name; the pleasure was so intense.

He kissed her then. A hard kiss. She was breathless. Dizzy with delight. She cupped his cheeks in fervid desire, drinking in the rich taste of him, the spicy scent of him.

"Say it again," he ordered, thrusting a second finger inside her moist womb.

"Oh, Sebastian."

"And again," he said roughly, pumping his fingers deep within her, kissing her between commands.

"Sebastian!" she cried again, and again, and again.

The most demanding pressure thrummed at her apex: a tension, so great, she wanted to scream in pleasure. She didn't dare, though. Instead, she groaned, telling Sebastian she was on fire, that she needed to be doused—and his fingers, blessedly, worked their magic.

Her muscles shuddered in gratification. She gasped at the spastic pulses. And then she let out a deep, long sigh—and settled on the settee, so sated, so full of joy.

Sebastian didn't seem able to stir much, either. And it was a long while before either one of them could say a word.

He kissed the tip of her nose. "I think you owe me something, Henry."

Dazed, Henrietta said, "Thank you."

He chuckled. "I appreciate the sentiment, Henry, but it's not what I had in mind."

She wrinkled her brow. "Then what?"

He gave her a roguish smile. "I do believe you owe me your baby toe."

She gasped again. "You *heard* me at the ball?!"

"Are you angry, Henry?"

She sighed. "I suppose not." She stuck out her bare foot. "Take it. It's yours."

He looked at the foot, bent down, and kissed the baby toe.

Henrietta smiled, pleased with his romantic gesture.

"Come." He scooped her in his arms, blanket and all, and collected a candle. "I'll take you back to your room."

With a sigh of contentment, Henrietta rested her head against the groove of his neck and closed her eyes.

It'd been perfect, the kiss. It was everything she had ever dreamed about. She was now surer than ever that Ravenswood was her mate in life. And after tonight's passionate encounter, she was just as sure he'd ask for her hand before Twelfth Night.

CHAPTER 13

Sebastian set the light aside before he placed Henrietta on the bed. In the shadows she looked a wanton sight. Hair rumpled. Eyes moist. Lips plump, still swollen after a sinfully delightful kiss.

His body ached with impotent lust. He wanted to touch her; to finish what they'd started in the library. But he fisted his palm, instead. He couldn't ruin the chit. He'd have to marry her then. And he damned well wasn't going to do that!

He bent down to buss her brow. "Goodnight, Henry."

She cupped his face in her soft palms and squeezed. "You don't have to go, Sebastian."

He was tempted. So very tempted by her seductive offer.

It baffled him, the intensity of his desire for her. He was a jaded wastrel. How could an innocent flower bewitch him so? There was something about Henrietta that inflamed the darkest recess of his soul. Her beauty, her goodness engaged him. Made the rogue within him stand up and take notice.

Sebastian settled on the bed beside her. He stroked the long and silky strands of her auburn hair scattered across the bedspread. In the candlelight, the russet locks glowed like the fiery streaks of a sunset. Her eyes, too, blazed in the smoldering light, perusing him with passion.

"You're so beautiful, Henry."

She lifted her lips to his. "So are you." And kissed him softly.

Sebastian closed his eyes with a faint groan. He slipped his hand beneath her head to support her, fingers curled in her rich mane, giving her freedom to ravish his mouth. She tasted like jasmine and he breathed in the fragrance, let it tease and enchant his senses.

"So beautiful," he said against her lips. "So good."

She opened her mouth for him. He slipped his wicked tongue between her teeth, stroking her. And when she moaned, a deep, feral moan, blood rushed through his veins, pulsed in his head, and pounded in his groin.

"Oh, Sebastian."

He deepened the kiss. He wasn't going to bed the girl. Really, he wasn't. He'd bring the kiss to surcease. Soon. He just wanted to taste her a little longer; to feel the warmth of her body. It both soothed his soul and rankled his lust, to have her pressed against him, writhing in sensual pleasure.

"Touch me," she bade.

He groaned again. Did she have to sound so sexy, his little despot? How was he supposed to wrest himself away from her if she beckoned—ordered—him to touch her? He damned well couldn't resist such an invitation. And he was beginning to think she knew it.

Sebastian stroked her waist, rubbed her rounded hip.

Henrietta cupped his hand and pushed it down. "Touch me lower, Sebastian."

The look of lust in her eyes made the blood pound in his cock. He was shaking, deuce it! Shaking like a virginal mooncalf. Henrietta was just so warm and sweet and so full of passion. He could stay in her arms forever.

It was a frightening thought.

Sebastian fixed his eyes to her flushed features. He didn't dare look down as she raked the train of her night rail over her knees. He'd lose every last ounce of resistance. Instead, he let her guide his hand to the moist crevice between her thighs; let her steer his fingers over the folds of her feminine flesh in any way that she wanted.

Sebastian dropped his brow to hers, pressed his lips to hers, breathing in the wanton sounds of her desire. He wanted nothing more than to tear the blasted shirt off his back; unfasten the buttons of his trousers and slip between Henrietta's warm and creamy thighs.

"Henry, you vixen."

He kissed her hard, stroked the petal soft skin between her legs.

The sweat dripped off his brow. He ached to bury himself deep inside her. It burned within him, the need to bed her.

In the passionate tussle, Sebastian's hand moved under her pillow—and knocked something hard.

He fingered the peculiar item. "What is this?"

He yanked the heavy object from its hiding spot.

A book.

Henrietta reached for it. "No, Sebastian!"

In the struggle, the tome landed on the bedside rug—and opened.

Sebastian bristled.

There, under flickering candlelight, was an image of fornication.

Sebastian sat up. Lust still raged in his groin, but the bewildering picture spread out at his feet captivated him.

He picked up the book and moved away from the bed. Taking in deep and steady drafts of air, he leafed through the tome.

Erotic picture after erotic picture passed before his eyes—and inflamed his passions even more.

"Where did you get this, Henry?"

She sat up, hair and wrapper rumpled, eyes wide. She curled her legs under her chin, and pulled the blanket up to her knees. "Well, I ... um ..."

"Tell me!"

She flinched.

He quickly regretted his clipped tone. But deuces, he was stunned. *What* was the girl doing with such a wonton tome?

"It was a gift," she said.

The lust still thrumming through his veins ebbed away, a simmering rage coursing through him instead.

"A gift?" A profound need to snap the impudent man's throat overwhelmed him. "From who? Tell me, Henry. Are you having an affair?"

"No!"

"Is he trying to seduce you? Give me his name. I'll kill him."

"There is no one, Sebastian. I swear."

He was breathing hard, ragged. "Then *who* gave you the book?"

"Madam Jacqueline."

She whispered the name. A woman's name.

Sebastian's mind raced. He had heard that name before. But where? And then it came to him. "The courtesan?"

Henrietta nodded.

"But why did you accept a gift from a courtesan?"

"You don't understand. I went to see Madam Jacqueline. I needed her help."

"For *what*?"

Silence.

"Out with it, Henry. Are you enceinte? Is that why you went to see the prostitute? To get rid of the babe?"

Her fists pounded on the bed. "How dare you, you stubborn blackguard! You know there isn't anyone in the world I want, but you!"

It was a blow to the gut, the revelation. Sebastian looked back at the book; to a picture of a woman straddling a man, dominating him … seducing him.

Nonplussed, Sebastian lifted his gaze to Henrietta. She had studied the book. It was evident in her very manner.

She had looked at the pictures, over and over again, dreaming up ways to bewitch him.

But still, she had refined her sexual allure in a short period of time. Even looking at sinful pictures was not enough to shape her carnal ways so quickly. She'd had a teacher.

His nostrils flared. "Tell me why you went to see Madam Jacqueline."

"Sebastian," she said more softly, "I needed her to teach me how to …"

"Say it, Henry!"

She huffed. "How to seduce you."

There it was, the dreaded truth.

"You tricked me," he breathed, even more bewildered. He had abandoned his home, drifted across the Continent for six months, all in the hope of breaking his bond with Henrietta. And *she* had plotted and schemed to seduce him the entire time he was away.

"No, Sebastian." She tossed the blanket aside and clambered to her knees. "I wanted to be with you. I didn't know how else to attract you."

He growled, "You mean you didn't know how else to trap me into marriage?"

A rush of memories flooded his head. It was all a ruse: her shapely hips and artful looks and whispered words. A bloody sham to enchant him. And she had risked her reputation, the fool girl, to learn the art of seduction. To leg-shackle him!

He slammed the book closed. "All that rubbish about friendship."

"But I did mean it, Sebastian. I *do* want to be your friend … and your lover."

He shuddered to hear her say the word "lover." She was a charming mess, her hair mussed, her wrapper askew. He could see the curves of her breasts, her hips beneath the flimsy night rail. Such a titillating sight, designed to entice him. To trap him—the poor, wicked viscount—into matrimony with the one thing he couldn't resist: sex.

Disbelief roiled in his belly. Wretched grief, too. Henrietta had betrayed him. He'd believed her the last good soul on earth. What tripe! He should have known there was no such thing as an innocent heart. After all, he spent much of his time cloistered amid the dregs of humanity. He understood the fickle human heart. And Henrietta was as devious as any other charlatan.

"You're just like all the other scheming flirts of the *ton*," he said.

"Sebastian, please." She crawled off the bed and limped to the bedpost, clutching it for support. "I did this for you."

He sneered, "For me?"

"Dash it, we belong together!"

"No, Henry, we do *not* belong together. We will *never* belong together."

She huffed. "Sebastian, I know you're angry, but listen to me."

He threw the book across the room. It collided with an armchair, the thud muffled.

"I've heard enough." He was fighting hard to keep his temper in check. One roaring word and he'd have the household at the door. Then he'd *have* to marry the conniving chit. "I'm leaving, Miss Ashby."

"Sebastian, wait!"

He thundered toward the door, opened it, then hastened into the corridor. It was late, so the passageway was deserted.

He headed for his room, his mind a whirl. He was such a bloody ass! How had he let the sly chit beguile him like that? She had so wholly bewitched him, he'd finally kissed her after four bloody years. He'd slathered his lips over her, groped her, shoved his fingers into her …

Sebastian stilled. He slumped against the cold wall and took in a sharp breath. He was a disgusting wretch. The girl might be a scheming flirt, but she was still an innocent. He had fingered the tightness of her sheath … and cupped the dewy folds of flesh at her apex.

He shuddered at the erotic memory and pushed away from the wall. He should not have tainted the girl with his vile touch. He should not have put his hands on her or his filthy mouth. And he definitely shouldn't have enjoyed the encounter so much.

Sebastian raked a shaky hand through his tousled mane. He had to leave the house. Pack his bags and never look back. He would go to his club. Relieve himself there of his burdensome lust. He was a fool for having touched the girl. But he was an even bigger fool for letting the scheming flirt charm him so.

"I will never forgive you for this, Henry."

CHAPTER 14

"Madam Jacqueline, I've ruined everything!"

Henrietta slumped against the cushioned divan, too distraught to even notice the courtesan was wearing her night rail and still tucked away in bed.

Tears gathered in Henrietta's eyes. Sickness roiled in her belly. She'd not nabbed a wink of sleep, so troubled by last night's stormy row. The fury in Sebastian's eyes haunted her still. The hurt, too.

She had to set things right. She had to make Ravenswood understand she was not just another fawning young miss, looking for a brilliant match. She loved him, the blackguard! So much so her heart ached at the thought of losing him.

"Good morning, Miss Ashby," said the courtesan.

It was a drab morning, so like the gloominess in Henrietta's heart. She looked up to say so, when she noticed the décor in the boudoir, all scarlet red in hue. Drapery … rugs … silk papered walls. All red. And then there was the bed. A bright red satin bedspread with flowing chiffon curtains framing the four wood posters. It was a big bed. And a small Madam Jacqueline was cozy under the covers, sitting up and reading the broadsheets.

"I'm sorry," said Henrietta. "I didn't think you were still in bed. The footman assured me I could come right up to speak with you."

Madam folded the newsprint in her lap. "You are welcome, Miss Ashby. Now tell me, what seems to be the trouble?"

Henrietta groaned. "Where to start?"

Madam Jacqueline patted the bed. "Come and sit by me."

Henrietta obeyed. She sat down at the foot of the bed, facing the courtesan.

Madam was draped in an elegant white night rail with rich embroidery. Her hair was hidden beneath a regal white turban, a striking diamond wedged in the center. The fair nightwear only highlighted her eerie mist green eyes, which captivated Henrietta the moment she settled next to the woman.

"What's happened, Miss Ashby?"

"It's Sebastian," she sobbed. "He hates me."

Madam Jacqueline eyed her shrewdly. "Why do you think he hates you?"

Henrietta took in a shaky breath before she recounted the entire wretched tale.

"If only he'd never found the naughty book of pictures," she said in closure, wiping the tears from her eyes.

The courtesan tsked. "I warned you not to be too zealous, Miss Ashby."

"I know," she said quietly. Ardent emotions frightened a man into retreat. So to find such a book in *her* room, to hear such a scandalous confession from *her* lips, that she had tried to seduce him, must have bowled Sebastian over. "How do I set things right, Madam Jacqueline?"

"Tell me, did Sebastian suspect you were seducing him before he found the book?"

"No, he looked so surprised when I told him."

"Then he is also very angry."

"Livid," said Henrietta, last night's row popping back into her head. She shivered at the memory, so cold. Sebastian had never treated her cruelly in all their years together. It was a terrible feeling, being cast aside like that.

"I tried to apologize. I tried to make him see I wasn't out to snag his title, his fortune."

"But he doesn't believe you?"

"No." Henrietta bowed her head. "He thinks I'm just another scheming flirt out to trap him into matrimony."

"I'm afraid he's going to stay angry with you for a very long time, Miss Ashby. He feels duped—by a woman. Most men find that humiliating."

Not the comforting words Henrietta was hoping to hear. "So I've lost him?"

"I wouldn't say that."

"Then there's hope?"

"You're going to have to apologize again."

"Oh, I'll say anything!" cried Henrietta. "Just tell me the right words!"

The courtesan shook her head. "You can't tell him in person. He will slam the door in your face, I'm afraid."

Henrietta slumped her shoulders forward. "So how will I tell him?"

"In a letter." Madam Jacqueline pointed to the desk. "Go to the vanity and collect a sheet of paper and quill."

Henrietta scrambled off the bed and hurried over to the cherrywood furniture. She plopped down on the quilted stool, snatched a quill from the ink well, and readied her hand.

"You must feel guilty," said Madam Jacqueline.

"Oh, I do," Henrietta vowed.

The courtesan waved her hand in a dismissive gesture. "It does not matter if you *really* feel guilty, Miss Ashby. You just have to sound remorseful."

Henrietta nodded.

"And you must inspire Sebastian to return to you; remind him of the night the two of you shared."

Yes, that's exactly what Henrietta wanted to do!

"Now I want you to write down every word I say," said Madam Jacqueline. "You will then deliver the letter to Sebastian and let *him* come to you when the time is right."

~ * ~

Henrietta hurried through the house, looking for Sebastian. She clutched the letter in her hand, grasping at hope that all was not lost between them.

At the end of the passageway was a staircase—at the top of the landing was Peter.

Henrietta darted up the steps, whilst Peter bounded down to her. The two met in the middle.

"Henry, I've been looking for you."

"I can't talk now, Peter." She brushed him aside. "I must find Ravenswood."

He gripped her arm, preventing her flight. "Henry, he's gone."

Her heart shuddered. "Gone where?"

"Back to London, I think. He left this morning in great haste."

She groaned. "Oh, no."

"What happened, Henry?"

There was no sense in keeping the secret from Peter. He was her ally, after all. She might as well confess the horrible happenstance to him.

"I made a blunder last night," she said

He offered her a kerchief. "What blunder?"

She sniffed and dabbed at her eyes with the napkin. "I tried to seduce him, Peter, but I failed."

He balked. "My dear, that was a rather bold move."

She sniffed again. "But I've been practicing for months."

This time he really looked ashen. "Good heavens, Henry, how?"

She recited the story about Madam Jacqueline: about Henrietta's transformation from fumbling novice to skilled seductress—well, perhaps not *that* skilled.

"Really?" Peter furrowed his brow. "But I never noticed a change in you."

"That's because I wanted to charm Sebastian, not you. You weren't supposed to notice anything different about me."

Peter took in a deep breath. "Well, we must find a way to right this matter."

Henrietta had already found a way: the letter. But now she had to find Sebastian so she could deliver it to him. She gripped her skirts in determination and mounted the steps again.

Peter fell in step behind her. "Where are you going, Henry?"

"To London."

"Oh, no." He followed her back to her room. "It's too dangerous."

But Henrietta dismissed his concern and set about gathering her things: a few toiletries to accommodate her on the short journey to London. She wasn't going to stay in Town for very long. She was going to deliver the letter, and then head home. She wasn't even going to meet with Sebastian. That was a definite faux pas, according to Madam Jacqueline. Henrietta was to slip the letter under Sebastian's door. And then wait. Wait for Sebastian to read the letter. Wait for his temper to cool. Wait for him to come to her. That was the plan.

"I'll take my maid with me," she said to reassure her alarmed brother-in-law.

"Your maid will not protect you from highwaymen, Henry."

Henrietta dropped a small trunk on the bed, and then dumped the toiletries inside. "Fine. I'll take you with me to London instead."

"No, Henry, *I'll* go to London," he said in a firm voice. "Alone. You stay here where it's safe."

She paused to glare at him. "I thought you wanted me to be with your brother?"

"I do."

"Then why are you trying to keep us apart?"

"I'm not, Henry." He moved to the other side of the bed. "It's dangerous on the road. It's better if I go and talk with Seb."

Henrietta mulled that over. Perhaps she should ask Peter to deliver the letter instead? After all, Sebastian was furious with her. It might be better if she steered clear of the city altogether.

But what if Peter lost the letter on the road? Or what if he forgot to give it to Sebastian once he reached London?

No, it was better if she delivered the letter. At least then she wouldn't wonder about the message, and if it had ever reached Sebastian.

Henrietta shook her head. "I have to go to London, Peter. I have to set things right."

"But you'll never find him once you reach London."

"Rot." She stuffed a fur-trimmed hat into the trunk. "I know where he lives."

"He won't be home, Henry. I'm sure of it."

"Oh?" A pair of boots next. "And where will he be?"

Peter raked a hand through his black hair. "There's this place on the Thames near Marlow: an abbey."

Henrietta cringed. "Oh no, Sebastian's going to become a monk! I never thought my seducing him would upset him *that* much." She tossed a dress into the trunk without a thought to the wrinkles. "I have to hurry!"

Peter lifted his hands. "No, Henry, he's not going to become a monk."

A fluttery sigh of relief. "Then what is he doing at the abbey?"

"He sometimes visits the abbey. It's … Oh, never mind. The point is the friars are very strict. They will not permit a lady inside the cloister."

Henrietta snorted. She would just skulk inside the abbey then. She'd been doing that a lot of late, sneaking in and out of houses to visit Madam Jacqueline. An abbey would be no different. She would slip the letter under Sebastian's cell door, then skirt away.

"Henry, stop." Peter reached over the bed and took her by the wrist. "You cannot go after Sebastian. Let me deal with my brother."

Henrietta was about to argue, but the stubborn gleam in Peter's eyes reminded her so much of Sebastian.

After a lengthy pause, she huffed. "Oh, all right."

"Promise me, Henry, you will *not* chase after Sebastian."

She crossed her fingers behind her back. "I promise."

CHAPTER 15

"Where are we, Miss Ashby?"

Henrietta peered out the window at a large abbey with spiked towers and hideous gargoyles. A row of yew trees framed the path leading to the abbey door, and a tall iron gate bordered the wooded property.

"We're at an abbey, Jenny."

Her maid sniffed from the cold. "Why are we here?"

"I have to deliver a letter."

"To whom, Miss Ashby?"

"To someone important," she returned in a soft vein.

The abbey appeared deserted. There were no lights flickering through the windows, even though it was late afternoon. Perhaps the friars had retired early to bed? She hoped so. It would make things much easier for her. She could sneak inside the abbey without disturbing anyone and deliver the letter.

"Wait here, Jenny."

The maid grabbed her forearm. "Miss Ashby, no!"

Henrietta patted her hand in a reassuring gesture. "Don't fret, Jenny. I won't be gone long. I promise."

The girl sighed. "Yes, Miss Ashby."

Henrietta tossed aside the fur blanket and stepped out of the boxed cutter. The snow crunched beneath her boots. She slipped on her gloves and lifted her hood before she bid the driver to wait. She then hoisted the sides of her skirts and trudged through the snow.

The gate was unlocked. A boon! She hadn't the dexterity to scale the iron fence. She peeled back the barred door, the icy hinges creaking. She winced. In the eerie calm the noise echoed like a ghostly cry.

She slipped through the gate and followed the snowy path. The looming trees hovered above her; their twisted branches sagged with snow. It was like hiking through a dark tunnel, and she shivered at the chilling shadows.

When she reached the abbey door, Henrietta glanced at the motif carved into the lintel: *Do as thou wilt.*

Odd. Not the religious greeting she'd expected from an abbey. But Henrietta hadn't come to contemplate dogma. She reached for the door latch ... It, too, was unlocked.

This is too easy, she thought, as she stepped into the friary. She'd anticipated more resistance. Peter had vowed the friars were strict; that they did *not* permit women inside the abbey. So why was the door unbarred?

Oh, well. She needn't fret too much about it. She was inside the abbey. That was all that mattered.

As she skirted through the great hall, she heard the distant hum of male voices. The monks must be having dinner. And Sebastian was with them, surely. Now how was she going to find his room?

She could always peek inside each of the cells, she supposed. If the friars were gathered for a feast, their rooms should be empty. Henrietta could just sneak from cell to cell, looking for Sebastian's things. After all, the friars weren't likely to have fine woolen breeches and gold-threaded waistcoats. It should be easy enough to spot Sebastian's fine apparel.

Henrietta roamed the hall, looking for doors or passages that might lead to the friars' private rooms, but it was too gloomy to see anything.

She waited for her eyes to adjust to the darkness, and just as a passageway came into view, more voices murmured outside the abbey door.

A panicked Henrietta dashed into a corner—and collided with a stone statue. She ducked behind the edifice, just before the door burst open.

Light streamed into the murky abbey.

An inebriated gentleman stumbled inside, lantern in hand. A dandy of the highest order. And on each arm was a … nun?

Long black habits draped the giggling girls.

Girls?

Giggling?

Henrietta pinched her brow. What was going on?

She eased out of her hiding spot and rested her palm on the cold surface of the icon for support. She quickly recoiled, though, and covered her mouth to keep from shrieking.

To her horror was the smooth expanse of a woman's bare bottom!

Henrietta eyed the blasphemous image in the dwindling light. The woman was perched on her hands and knees, legs spread wide, posterior thrust in the air.

Henrietta had seen this kind of image before, in her naughty book of pictures. But *what* was it doing in an abbey hall?

The trio of peculiar characters stumbled through the passageway, taking the sole source of light with them.

What is this place?

It wasn't a true abbey, a place of refuge, so *what* was Sebastian doing here?

Henrietta was determined to learn the answer. She scurried after the cohorts, keeping a good distance behind them. At the end of the passage was a stone staircase, winding to an underground chamber.

Her heartbeat surged as she watched the besotted troupe hobbled down the steps. She raked her teeth over her bottom lip. Perhaps she should turn around and go home? Forget about the abyss beckoning below?

But boisterous cackles drifted up the spiral passageway, and Henrietta was firmly fixed on the idea of snooping some more. She *had* to know what was happening in the depths of the abbey. She had to know what *Sebastian* was doing in the depths of the abbey.

She pressed her hand to the rough stone wall … and made her way into the abyss. As she neared the landing, torchlight revealed a narrow enclosure. She soon spotted a rack of habits dangling from hooks along the wall. Quickly she confiscated a black robe and slipped it over her mantle to hide her identity. She then entered another corridor.

More stone statues lined the tunnel—clothed, thank heavens—their stone faces veiled, their lips stuffed with gauze. No eyes? No mouth? What did it mean? One wasn't supposed to see or speak about the abbey? Of the goings on inside?

Henrietta followed the echo of spirited laughter. At the end of the passage, the hilarity boomed.

She stopped at the threshold of a great round hall, alight with torches. She placed her gloved hand over her mouth again, stifling a horrified gasp.

Strapped to a long wood table was a woman—a naked woman!—her arms stretched high above her head, her legs spread wide.

Henrietta clutched her queasy belly. A terrible fright gripped her. The shackled woman didn't seem alarmed, though, even with a horde of masked and heckling misfits surrounding her, groping her. In truth, she was howling right alongside her admirers.

Henrietta grabbed the wall for support, vertigo brushing over her. She stared, stunned, as the men poured wine over the naked woman, squeezed fruit juice over her belly, then lapped up the sticky contents, using the woman as a plate.

It was a ghastly sight.

Henrietta pressed her back against the wall, hiding in the shadows. She skulked through the arena, desperate to find Ravenswood, to understand why he was here among such madness.

"Well, hullo, luv."

She bristled. She looked up to find a masked stranger, blond curls mussed, breath tainted with spirits, blocking her path.

"You're a pretty little nun." He stroked her trembling chin with his knuckle. A purple mask with plumes covered his face, all except his eyes: dark green eyes, ever so cold. He said with a spurious smile, "Perhaps we should put you on the banquet table next?"

Appalled by the very thought, Henrietta stomped on his foot.

He yelped.

She skirted around him, dashing across the arena. She had to find Sebastian. She had to get out of this disgusting place!

Henrietta darted into another dark tunnel. She was tempted to scream Sebastian's name and be done with it. To hell with Madam Jacqueline's rule; Henrietta didn't care anymore if Sebastian spotted her. She just wanted to get out of the catacombs—and to take the viscount with her.

But how was she going to find him in this dark hell?

Henrietta traipsed through the unfamiliar tunnels, and cringed when she heard so many rowdy voices behind so many closed doors. After months of analyzing Madam Jacqueline's naughty book of pictures, it didn't take much to imagine what was going on in the cells.

Henrietta stilled.

She recognized that male voice!

She pressed her ear to one of the doors, but her pulse was thumping so loud in her head, she couldn't hear the goings on.

She had to be sure, though.

Henrietta reached for the latch and opened the door just a tad.

Her belly lurched.

Sebastian stood in the room, eyes closed, head back. He was fully clothed, but for his open trouser flaps. At his feet was a woman—a nun!—taking him into her mouth.

Henrietta screamed.

Sebastian's head snapped up. "*Henry!*" he roared.

Henrietta staggered back, bumping into the damp wall. Bile roiled in her belly. She quickly hiked up her skirts and dashed back through the tunnel, into the noisy arena.

"Henry, stop!" a voice boomed behind her.

She struggled out of the arena, ignoring that powerful voice, frantic. She ripped off the habit, and blinded by tears, scaled the winding stairs, desperate to escape the gruesome catacombs.

She wanted to scream and pound the floor. To lash out in grief. Her every step was weighed by the burden of her broken heart.

Henrietta made her way to the abbey door. She burst through it, into the winter night. She took one step, then two before the nausea overwhelmed her and she retched into the pure white snow.

Hot tears stained her cheeks. She staggered down the path, looking for the gate. She opened her mouth to call for Jenny, but a sob came out instead.

"Henry!"

She shuddered to hear him say her name. "Get away from me!"

Sebastian grabbed her, squeezed her arms. "What are you doing here, Henry?"

"Me!" She squirmed in his embrace. "What are *you* doing here?"

"Don't evade the question." He gave her shake. "Answer me!"

"I came to give you this." She pushed the letter into his chest. He let her go and grabbed the paper. "I wanted to set things right between us, but I'm such a fool!"

"You shouldn't have come here, Henry."

"What is this place?" she cried, wiping the tears from her eyes.

"My club."

"Your club?" she sneered. "This is where you gather with your friends?" She pointed at the abbey. "What kind of a hell is that?"

"Just that, Henry, the Hellfire Club."

A vile name indeed. "You meet in an abbey?"

"Our founder had the abbey restored more than seventy years ago."

"This has been going on for *decades*?"

Years of debauchery. Years of fiendish pursuits. And Sebastian was a part of it all. He wallowed in the decadence, the depravity. He *liked* it!

The ache tore at her heart.

"Is this what you do for pleasure, Sebastian? Celebrate vice?"

He was silent.

"*Why?*" she cried.

He took a step toward her, shoved the letter in his pocket, then grabbed her by the arms again. "Some of us are born good, Henry, and some of us are born damned. I wasn't born good, and I'm not going to fight fate."

She gasped. "Rot!" She twisted her arms to break free of his hold. "You have a choice, Sebastian. You *don't* have to come here."

He let her loose; raked a shaky hand through his thick and wavy hair. "Henry—"

"Who are the men inside?" she demanded, tears still burning her cheeks.

He was breathing hard. "Men like me, Henry."

"The *ton* you mean?" She croaked, "And you bed *nuns*?"

"Not nuns, Henry. Doxies dressed like nuns."

So that was it. No *ladies* allowed, but doxies …

No wonder Peter had tried to stop her from coming to the abbey. He'd wanted to spare her from the hideous sight of his ignoble brother.

"But where are the friars?" she said. "Peter told me there were friars."

"Peter?"

Henrietta sensed she had rankled him even more with the confession about his brother, but she was too grieved to care. She just wanted answers, hurtful as they might be. Her world was shattering around her, but she still wanted more from Sebastian. She wanted more truth.

Sebastian took a moment of repose before admitting, "We are the friars."

"Oh, I see." She sniffed. "The 'friars' bed the 'nuns' in the abbey." It was enough to make her retch again, admitting the words aloud. "You're a fiend."

"I know, Henry."

But she didn't know. That was the wretched truth. For four years she'd loved, even worshipped, a fantasy. Sebastian wasn't a gallant knight. He was a villain, just as her sisters had warned. And *she* had adored him. Seduced him. Wanted to *marry* him!

Oh God, it hurt, the candor. It hurt so much she wanted to scream again. He looked so formidable in the shadows. So wicked. So *un*like her Sebastian. The hero she had dreamed up in her head.

"I want you to stay away from me," she sobbed. "Don't ever come near me again!"

"I won't," he said quietly. "I promise."

CHAPTER 16

Sebastian returned to the banquet hall. He grabbed a bottle of rum, popped the cork and guzzled the liquid fire.

He had finally shattered Henrietta's girlhood fancy for him. It was a deuced shame she'd learned the truth about him in such a vile manner, but the deed was done.

Sebastian dropped into a chair and took another swig of rum, trying to blot out the memory of Henrietta's tears.

She'd recover from the shock soon enough, he reckoned. She was a charming—though misguided—chit with a predisposition for daydreaming about knights and princes. She'd find herself a deserving beau next season, and Sebastian would be dismissed from her mind like a bad dream.

Bloody rum! Not working fast enough. A cutting pain speared his chest; squeezed his lungs, making it hard to breathe.

There would be no more adoring looks or spirited laughter or passionate kisses. He was free from the girl. He needn't pretend he was a gallant gentleman anymore. He was free to be the man he was always destined to be—a villain—a wicked villain who'd just squashed Henrietta's heart.

Sebastian rubbed his aching temples. What had possessed the girl to come to the abbey in the first place?

The letter.

He fumbled through his pocket, searching for the cursed piece of paper. He found it in the lining of his coat, all crumpled up.

He unfurled the message:

Dear Sebastian,

It grieves me terribly, the hurt that I have caused you. When I think of last night, the warmth of your breath on my lips, the rampant beats of both our hearts, I am filled with remorse at the thought of losing all that is good between us. Forgive me.

Yours,
Henry

Sebastian stared at the letter, the words sinking into his sloshed brain. All that was good between them? Aye, it had been good … But the girl didn't want his forgiveness anymore.

His vision finally fogged. About bloody time! The bright torchlight, the besotted friars, the moans of wenches all mix together in his head. He beckoned the darkness to come, to stomp asunder the misery in his gut. Instead, the natter of a pest disturbed his drunken stupor.

"She was mine, Ravenswood." The chap slurred his words as he took a seat opposite Sebastian. "You'd no right to take her from me."

Sebastian trained his wavering gaze to the grating mooncalf, but all he could see were purple feathers.

"Who are you?" snarled the viscount.

The mooncalf fumbled with the laces of his mask.

"Emerson," the viscount gritted.

A young upstart, Emerson was the son of an earl. He had joined the Hellfire Club to obtain a notorious reputation—and thus ruffle his officious father's feathers. Perhaps he even wanted to send the earl into an early grave with the shock of his "infamous" ways?

What rot! Emerson infamous? He was a peevish misfit with an iniquitous cruel streak. Like the other friars in the club, he was a coward, too timid to show his face more'n half the time.

It was bloody absurd in Sebastian's estimation. If one didn't *really* enjoy ignominy, one shouldn't join a society like the Hellfire Club. Wearing a mask was a timorous pretense.

"What the deuces are you talking about, Emerson? What woman?"

"The spirited wench you just chased after."

Sebastian hardened.

"She was mine, Ravenswood." Emerson pointed to his chest. Missed. And poked himself in the throat. "I'd picked her."

"Picked her for what?" Sebastian growled.

"To be our next banquet, o'course. Mmm." He licked his lips. "She'd have made a tasty dish, strapped to the table—"

The besotted Emerson shrieked.

Sebastian shot out of his chair, gripped by a pounding fury, fists swinging. But vertigo nearly plunked him back into his seat.

Emerson, meanwhile, toppled out of his chair, and scurried on hands and knees to get away from the ominous viscount.

Sebastian gathered his composure and set off after the rabble-rouser, knocking chairs and tables out of his way.

The friars erupted in hoarse guffaws, clamoring, "Go get 'im, Ravenswood!"

Emerson scrambled under the banquet table. It was a sturdy structure, too heavy for Sebastian to tip. Instead, the viscount stomped to the other side of the table and grabbed the cowering wastrel by the ankles.

Emerson let out another holler and kicked.

Sebastian, thoroughly foxed, lost his hold on the scalawag, who disappeared into one of the tunnels.

Sebastian could feel the darkness clawing at his eyes. And why was he chasing after Emerson again? He didn't remember anymore.

He staggered into a nearby tunnel and stumbled into an empty cell. He collapsed on the bed as darkness finally overwhelmed him.

~ * ~

Meanwhile, on the other side of the catacombs, a distraught Emerson had curled into a quiet corner, the stinging tears of humiliation burning his cheeks. He didn't have a contusion on his body, but the bruise to his ego was sore indeed.

The ring of laughter still echoed in his ears. The friars' sporting taunts. He was disgraced. He could never return to the Hellfire Club. And all because of that savage brute, Ravenswood. Emerson didn't know what had set off the viscount, but he was determined to make the man suffer.

Dearly.

But how?

A scrap of paper caught the besotted Emerson's eye. The same scrap of paper Ravenswood had been reading before he'd stomped after him like an ogre. The viscount must have lost the letter in the fury of the chase. It was now wedged under a chair leg, fluttering in the cold catacomb breeze.

Emerson crawled back into the banquet hall and snatched the letter from its precarious spot.

He skulked back into the tunnel, away from the bacchanal, and read the letter.

The words danced on the page. He was foxed. He had to concentrate hard to get the inscription to stay still and make some sort of sense.

After a few deep breaths and a hard stare, he deciphered the content.

A love note!

He scrolled further down the missive.

From a *man*!

Emerson had never suspected Ravenswood to be the type to consort with a man. Henry, was it? What a fabulous piece of *on-dit*! It will surely ruin the knave once word leaked out.

Emerson cast his wavering gaze over the crowd of inebriated friars. He tried to remember their names. Was there a Henry among the rowdy lot?

But wait ... Ravenswood had chased after a harlot earlier in the night. The very harlot Emerson had wanted to strap to the banquet table. And hadn't Ravenswood called her ... Henry?

Could Henry be a woman?

But who would name a woman Henry?

Blast it! Emerson rubbed his throbbing temples. He'd had too much to drink. He couldn't think straight.

But soon a name dawned on him. Henry ... as in Henrietta Ashby, the eccentric daughter of Baron Ashby. There was much buzz about the flamboyant family. Could she be the woman in the letter?

Emerson was going to find out. And then he would have his revenge. If the chit was in love with the viscount—and Ravenswood wanted nothing to do with her—it would be the greatest form of punishment, to make him marry the very woman he loathed. And he loathed the wench; it was clear. He'd chased her from the abbey, hollering the entire time. He'd hate to be leg-shackled to the wench for the rest of his days. But what choice would he have once the scandal broke? She was the daughter of a baron; Ravenswood would have to save her reputation. And spend the rest of his life in misery.

Perfect.

CHAPTER 17

Henrietta stumbled on the first step. Wretched tears! She was desperate to reach her room and crawl under the bedcovers. She wanted to forget all about Sebastian; that the man was a fiend. She wanted to forget she had tried to seduce that fiend; that she had loved that fiend.

"Ugh," she cried, staggering again.

She had sobbed the entire journey home. And she was exhausted. She had nothing left but a broken heart.

"Henry!"

"Leave me alone, Peter."

Peter bounded after her and grabbed her arm. "Henry, I've been waiting for you to come home. You went after him, didn't you? What happened? Did he hurt you?"

She jerked her arm away. "He devastated me!"

Peter looked devastated himself. "Henry, I'm so sorry."

"Why didn't you tell me, Peter?"

"I warned you not to go after him."

"No, I mean *why* didn't you tell me he was a fiend?"

Peter raked a shaky hand through his hair. "I thought you could save him, Henry."

"He's a monster! And you didn't even warn me. You wanted me to *marry* him!"

"He's not all bad, Henry. He just needs someone to care for; someone to care about him."

She pointed to her chest. "Well, it's not going to be me."

Henrietta bumped into her eldest sister at the top of the landing.

"What's going on?" said Penelope, glancing from her husband to Henrietta. "Henry, where have you been?"

Henrietta brushed past her sister and rushed into her room. She flopped onto the bed and embraced her pillow … but the fabric smelled like Eau de Cologne.

Last night, she had snuggled with Sebastian in this very bed. She could still feel the warmth of his breath on her skin, feel the soft touch of his lips, see the smoldering look in his eyes. He had been so tender, yet passionate. So much like the hero she had dreamed about for *four* long years.

Henrietta tossed the pillow across the room. She grabbed the covers, buried her face in the quilt, and bumped her head against Madam Jacqueline's naughty book of pictures. In a fit of pique, she tossed that, too—under the bed—where it wouldn't cause anymore trouble.

"Henry?"

Penelope stood in the doorway, dressed in her wrapper, frowning in consternation.

Henrietta's bottom lip started to tremble. "You were right, Penelope. Ravenswood is nothing but a rogue."

Penelope quickly clambered onto the bed. "Come here, sweet."

Henrietta slumped against her sister and wailed into Penelope's breast until she was sapped of tears. She didn't even notice the other hands that stroked her hair and caressed her back. Or the depression in the bed as three more sisters gathered around her in support. All Henrietta could feel was a throbbing ache in her chest: an ache she feared would never go away.

~ * ~

Henrietta stared at her reflection in the mirror. She looked different. Older? She certainly felt different. Even the world around her had changed. It was less bright. Less hopeful.

"Leave my hair down today, Jenny."

The maid nodded. "Yes, Miss Ashby."

Jenny picked up the hairbrush and combed it through Henrietta's tangled hair. She tugged at the locks to unravel the knots.

Henrietta tried to unravel some knots, too. Knots in her heart. All sorts of distressing thoughts came to mind, though, consumed her concentration.

Thoughts of Sebastian.

He haunted her dreams, disturbed her waking hours. She was determined to be rid of him; her heart was still clinging to him.

Foolish heart! When would it learn? The world wasn't filled with heroes and knights. It was peppered with villains and an assortment of worthy men. Henrietta had to sift through the lot of scoundrels to find one such worthy man. But whoever he might be, he was not Ravenswood.

Jenny finished braiding Henrietta's hair just as the bedroom door opened.

Henrietta looked over her shoulder. "Good morning, Mama. I'll be ready for breakfast in just a minute."

Henrietta was late—as usual—but it was unlike the baroness to be so impatient about her tardiness. In fact, it was family tradition to start the meal without her. So why had Mama come to fetch her?

"Jenny, I would like to speak with my daughter—alone."

Jenny bobbed a curtsy. "Yes, my lady." And she skirted from the room.

Henrietta watched the girl shut the bedroom door, then returned her attention to her mother. "What's the matter, Mama? Why did you shoo Jenny from the room?"

The baroness approached her youngest daughter with a sheet of paper and quill pen. "Because there are some things a servant should not hear."

Henrietta lifted a brow. "Such as?"

"Would you like satin or taffeta for your wedding dress?"

Henrietta paled. "Wedding dress?"

"And lilies are your favorite bloom, are they not? I shall put in an order for a hundred lilies at the hot house. No, two hundred."

Henrietta started to feel dizzy "Lilies?"

"Now let's talk about the wedding menu."

Alarmed, Henrietta grabbed her belly. "*What* wedding, Mama!"

With a very innocent air, the baroness quipped, "Why yours, Henry. Now don't dawdle. We have much to do before Twelfth Night."

"Twelfth Night!" Henrietta sailed out of her chair. "But the marriage license?"

"Being fetched as we speak."

The room was spinning. "Who am I marrying?"

"Your betrothed, of course ... Viscount Ravenswood."

Henrietta grabbed the back of the chair, feeling queasy. "Mama, what's happening?"

"It's very simple, my dear. You've disgraced yourself and now you must pay the consequences."

A lump formed in Henrietta's throat and burning tears filled her eyes.

"Now don't blubber, Henry." The baroness sashayed over to the vanity and picked up a lacy kerchief. She shoved it under her daughter's nose. "We have to get back to the matter at hand. Shall we serve goose or duck at the wedding luncheon?"

"Mama, I—"

"Goose it is. Now how about the soup? Pheasant, perhaps?"

Henrietta twisted the kerchief around her finger. "I don't want to marry Ravenswood."

"You don't have a choice, Henry."

"But I—"

The baroness touched Henrietta's lips, silencing her. "Perhaps you did not hear me, Henry. You've made a spectacle of yourself. The whole Town is in a tizzy about the shameful letter you wrote to Ravenswood. You are ruined. Your father is ruined. I am ruined. Your sisters and their husbands and their children are ruined. And you are going to marry Ravenswood and make it right. Is that understood?"

A great welter of shame stormed Henrietta's breast. The letter! "You know about the letter?"

"*Everybody* knows about the letter."

Grief and rage knotted together in Henrietta's belly. Ravenswood! That bastard! He couldn't just devastate her foolish fancy, he had to devastate her very respectability, too, by showing the letter all over Town?

Henrietta rushed to the window and pushed back the curtains.

Air! She needed air!

"Get ahold of yourself, Henry," the baroness chided. "We have to retore our family honor."

Henrietta pushed and pushed against the frozen pane of glass. The casement parted, at last. Cold winter air whooshed inside the room.

"Henry." The baroness hugged herself to ward off the chill. "Close that window at once!"

But Henrietta did no such thing. She stuck her head out the window and inhaled the biting wind, wishing the cold could numb her heart and the fury in her belly.

"Henry, you'll catch your death!"

Henrietta didn't care. In truth, marriage to Sebastian would be a death of a sort. To be leg-shackled to that villain for the rest of her days? She would be miserable. Forever.

"Enough of the dramatics, Henry." The baroness marched over to the window, yanked her daughter back inside the room, and closed the glass. "You didn't think

Ravenswood such a terrible match when you wrote him that letter."

"Mama, I—"

"I don't want to hear it, Henry. Oh, this is all your father's fault!" The baroness lifted her hands heavenward, as though in prayer, before she scooped up the side of her dress and flounced over to the hearth. "He reared you like a boy. But you are not a boy, Henry. You cannot act like one!"

"I know, Mama," she said quietly.

Lady Ashby made a noise of distress as she rubbed her hands together. "Then *what* possessed you to write such an outrageous letter?"

"I thought ..." Henrietta slowly dragged her feet over to the bed. She wrapped her arms around the bedpost and hugged the wood with all her might. "I thought he loved me, Mama. We had a fight. I thought if I wrote him the letter ..."

"All would be well again?" The baroness huffed. "Well, you got your wish, Henry. You're going to be the next Viscountess Ravenswood."

Henrietta shivered at the title: a title she did not want anymore. And Ravenswood had promised to stay away from her so, hopeful, she said, "He won't marry me, Mama."

"He most certainly will," the baroness proclaimed in a very pompous voice, "or there's going to be duel."

Henrietta gasped. The very thought of Ravenswood and Papa in an empty field in the wee hours of the morning had her heart fluttering in distress. "But Papa's a terrible shot!"

Lady Ashby pointed to her chest. "*I* would shoot him, Henry."

Henrietta supposed even a blackguard like Ravenswood would not duel with a woman, so there was no other way to settle the matter—she had to get married.

"But Ravenswood doesn't care for me, Mama."

And Henrietta didn't care for him. He was a blackguard, through and through. Oh God, what had she done! She should never have written that letter. She should never have visited with Madam Jacqueline. She had made such a terrible mess of her life. And now she was going to pay for her foolery.

Rightly so, she supposed. Who else should suffer but her? It was all her doing, all her wretched fault. And now her family was tainted by the scandal, too. What choice did she have but to marry Ravenswood? She had to save the family name, the honor of her parents and sisters. And she could not marry another, more respectable gentleman. Who would want her now, after such a disgrace? She had to marry. And she had to marry Ravenswood.

"Whether Ravenswood cares for you or not is inconsequential. The deed is done, Henry. You'd best prepare yourself for the wedding."

Henrietta slumped her brow against the bedpost, the horror of her dismal fate sinking into her brain. "Yes, Mama."

She was going to be Ravenswood's wife. A few days ago she would have been thrilled by the news, but today she was anything but. Just the thought of being the next Viscountess Ravenswood made her heart hurt. The rogue was going to spend his marital days at his fiendish club. He was not going to give up his wicked ways for her, she was sure.

And she would have to endure the humiliation of it all, the disgrace. Didn't the *ton* already whisper about his immoral pursuits? Her sisters had heard the ghastly rumors, so the gossip must be widespread. She was going to have to bear the snickers and the pity. And she was going to have to endure a daily reminder of her foolery. Each time she was near her husband, she would remember her childhood fancy: the noble hero she had invented in her head. And each time she would feel the shame of her silly girlhood dream.

The smarting pain on her chest made it hard to breathe. She had hoped to forget all about Ravenswood, to banish the villain from her heart and soul. She had hoped to find a better, more respectable husband. But both hopes were now dashed to bits.

"I can't believe I'm getting married," said Henrietta.

"Yes, it was a shock to us all. Your poor father almost had an apoplexy when he heard the news."

"Oh no, Papa!" Henrietta rushed to the door, panic knocking on her breast. "Is he all right?"

"Hold it right there, Henry!"

Henrietta froze with her hand on the door latch.

"Your father is napping and I don't want you to disturb him. It took me all morning to calm him down."

A wave of horrendous guilt washed over her. "Papa must loathe me."

"Loathe you?" The baroness snorted. "He adores you, Henry. He always will. He doesn't give a fig about the scandal."

Henrietta turned around to face her mother again. "Then why is he so upset?"

"Because you're getting married! Your papa believed you'd live the life of a spinster forever—with him. He's upset because he's losing you."

Henrietta simpered. "Then he doesn't hate me?"

"No, Henry. He doesn't hate you."

Relief filled Henrietta's heart. She had already lost Ravenswood, the hero she had dreamed up in her head. And if she had lost her papa's love, too, it would have been an unbearable blow.

"Do you hate me, Mama?"

The baroness was quiet for a moment, then said, "No, Henry. I don't hate you. But I'm very angry with you."

Henrietta bowed her head in shame. "I understand, Mama."

Lady Ashby sighed and opened her arms. "Come here, child."

Henrietta rushed into her mother's embrace and sobbed.

"There now, Henry. It will be all right. You'll see."

But Henrietta knew those words could not be true. Ravenswood was a blackguard. He would make her miserable.

"Perhaps we should talk about the wedding night, Henry."

Her corset suddenly seemed too tight, and Henrietta took in a deep breath to settle her nerves. She didn't need any instruction about the wedding night. Madam Jacqueline had made sure of that. But an alarming thought just entered her head: she was going to be Ravenswood's wife—in every sense of the word. And the wicked scoundrel had a delicious touch; she knew all about *that*, too.

Well, Henrietta would not tolerate his touch. She would not let the rogue play with her heart—or her body. He might soon be her husband, but Sebastian could go to the devil. Their marriage would be in name only. Let the lascivious bounder rut about with the "nuns" at his club. He would *never* touch her again!

CHAPTER 18

Sebastian opened his eyes. The room was spinning. He shut his eyes with a groan, willing the nausea in his belly to go away.

It was a few minutes of steady breathing before he flicked open his lashes again. Squinting, he focused on the familiar red and gold drapes and embroidered coverlet.

He was home.

How did he get here? Sebastian had no memory of the journey to his London town house.

Slowly he rolled to the edge of the bed and sat up. He rubbed his throbbing head. He was stiff and sore and dizzy.

But soon the fog in his brain lifted—and he saw Henrietta, standing under the yew trees, her cheeks stained with tears.

"Shit," he hissed, the memory of last night storming his brain.

That fierce ache in his breast returned, too. A bottle of rum had dulled the pain for a short time, but the charm of intoxication was starting to fade. Sober now, he was still haunted but the grief in Henrietta's eyes.

Blast it! She was a conniving chit, remember? She had tried to seduce him; beguile him into matrimony. He should wring the woman's neck for pulling such a stunt, not wallow in stifling guilt.

Sebastian lifted his head to look around the room. It was morning. He could see the sunlight peeking through the drapes. He could also sense another presence in the room.

He scanned the shadows in the bedchamber.

Nothing moved.

He trained his clouded vision on the furniture once more. And then he saw it, the figure in the armchair.

Sebastian grunted. "I suppose I have you to thank for bringing me home?"

Peter didn't say anything.

Sebastian glared at his brother. "And I suppose I have you to thank for telling Henrietta about the Hellfire Club?"

Sebastian couldn't hide the fury from his voice. If Peter had not betrayed the location of the abbey, Henrietta would never have stumbled upon him in such a compromising position. She would never have learned the truth about him in such a vile manner. She was a scheming flirt, true. But she needn't have witnessed him with the doxy. It was an unnecessary hurt; it would forever haunt him—and he loathed feeling remorse. It was deuced uncomfortable. And he had his brother to thank for everything.

"Say something, damn it!" Sebastian regretted his boisterous tone. It only exacerbated the pain in his head. He said with more temperance, "Don't just sit there."

Peter abandoned the armchair and crossed the room. He grabbed Sebastian by his shirt, pushed him to the bed, and shoved his knee under Sebastian's chin until he couldn't breathe or say a word.

"You miserable son of a bitch," Peter growled. "You just had to devastate Henry like that, didn't you? You're a black-hearted villain!"

Peter got off the bed and started to pace the room with quick, angry strides.

Sebastian shot up, wheezing, eager to pound his impudent brother into the floorboards. But vertigo knocked him off balance, and he slumped to his knees instead.

"Look at you," Peter sneered. "You can't even stand. Is this how you want to spend the rest of your days? On your knees, in a drunken stupor?"

Sebastian sucked in a deep breath, trying to stop the room from spinning in his eyes.

"And to think," said Peter, "I offered to help Henrietta win your heart."

"You bloody ass, you've been *helping* the chit seduce me?" He was going to kill his brother just as soon as he could stand. "Is that why you sent her to the abbey?"

"I didn't *send* her. I made the girl promise not to chase after you. She didn't listen, though."

Sebastian snorted. "Henry never listens."

"Yes, well, that might have been *my* mistake"—he pointed to his chest—"telling the girl about the abbey. But why did *you* have to ruin her?"

Sebastian sat on his heels. "What are you talking about?"

"The letter you so cruelly passed all over Town."

"What letter, damn it?"

Peter stopped pacing. "The love letter from Henry. You know, the one about your breath, your heart, and other such rot?"

A vague recollection filled Sebastian's besotted brain. "You know about the letter?"

"The whole Town knows about the letter! How could you be so ruthless, Seb? How could you flaunt that letter all over the city?"

"That's horseshit, Peter! I would never flaunt such a letter. And you damn well know it!"

"Oh, really?" Peter quirked a brow. "So how does the *ton* know about it?"

"Damned if I know. But I have the letter right here." Sebastian reached across the floor for his coat. He shoved his hand into the pocket and rummaged for the paper.

Empty.

"I did have it," Sebastian murmured.

"Well, now London's greatest gossips have it." Peter stalked across the room and flung open the heavy drapes.

Sebastian squinted at the blinding light.

Peter moved away from the window. "And Henrietta is ruined!"

Sebastian hardened. "What are you saying, Peter?"

He smiled, the daft man. "I'm offering to be the best man at your wedding, Seb."

Sebastian roared. "I will *not* marry the girl!" And right away the spasms started pounding in his head again.

Sebastian wanted to keel over and die.

"And why not?" demanded Peter.

"Because she tried to seduce me! Trick me into matrimony!"

Peter snorted. "Well, you didn't give her much choice in the matter, now did you?"

Sebastian blinked. He had not expected his brother to say that.

"You're stubborn, Seb. The girl was in love with you. You were acting the pigheaded fool, so what other choice did she have but to seduce you?"

Sebastian murmured, "I can't believe I'm hearing this."

"She risked everything, Seb, to be with you. She went to see a courtesan, for heaven's sake! She put her reputation in jeopardy, her very heart and soul. And all because she believed you were worth the risk."

"That was her foolish mistake."

"Do you really believe that? Or are you just being hardheaded again?"

Sebastian growled. "Get out, Peter, before I wring your neck."

He scoffed. "Don't play bully with me, Seb. I'll match you growl for growl."

What was the matter with Peter? He was always the more docile, accommodating brother; he rarely encouraged a confrontation. He certainly never started one!

Sebastian rubbed his aching brow. "What do you want from me, Peter?"

"Sober and hitched to Henrietta."

"That does it." Sebastian sprang to his feet, wavered, and hit the floor again, clutching his throbbing head. "Bloody hell."

Peter tsked. "Pull yourself together, Seb. The wedding will be on Twelfth Night."

"Like hell!"

"I'm off to fetch the marriage license myself."

Sebastian growled, "You treacherous son of a—"

"What are you afraid of, Seb?"

Sebastian glared at his brother, moving around in circles. "Stand still, damn it!"

"I am," Peter said dryly.

Sebastian humphed.

"Well, Seb?"

Peter crossed his arms over his chest. He looked so much like Father when he did that, all officious and stern. It sent a shiver down Sebastian's spine.

What were they talking about again? "Well what, Peter?"

"*Why* are you afraid to be with Henrietta?"

"Rot!" He snorted. "She's a scheming flirt, and I *don't* want her for my wife. How do I know *she* didn't show that letter all over Town, just to trap me into marriage? She could have come back to the catacombs, after I'd passed out, and stolen the letter from my pocket."

Peter snorted. "I think I can assure you she did no such thing."

"I wouldn't put it past the devious chit. And why are *you* so sure she's innocent?"

Sebastian gripped the bed for support, struggling to stand. But he failed and dropped back onto the bed.

"Because the girl hates you." Peter walked over to the armchair and collected his gloves. "No one is happy about the approaching wedding, Seb, least of all Henry. She did *not* orchestrate this scandal, I assure you."

Sebastian wasn't prepared for the stabbing pain in his chest.

Peter slipped on his gloves. "You made quite an impression on the girl at the abbey. She doesn't give a fig whether you live or die anymore. Bravo, brother!"

Despite the pang in his breast, Sebastian gritted, "Good."

"I'm glad you think so." Peter moved to collect his greatcoat. "Now about the wedding …"

"Blast it, I haven't agreed—"

"Are you really going to leave Henry—and her *whole* family—in disgrace?"

Sebastian was sorely tempted to let the conniving chit stew in her own foolery, but deep down he knew he would never really leave her in ignominy. Angry as he was at the girl, he could not abandon her in shambles. He had known Henrietta for far too long to just desert her at such a grim time.

"She should never have written that silly letter," Sebastian grumbled.

"No, she shouldn't have, but the deed is done. I'll summon the tailor to get started on the wedding clothes."

Sebastian sighed in defeat. "Blast it all to hell!"

"It's your life, Seb. Are you really determined to be miserable?"

"And what other choice do I have? I'm being forced to marry!"

"Yes, that's true." Peter slipped on his greatcoat. "The wedding is going to take place whether you like it or not, so that's why I suggest you make the best of it."

"And how do I do that?"

Peter picked up his top hat. "Well, perish the thought you try to get along with the girl—your betrothed."

"What a ghastly word."

"Well, here's another ghastly word for you" your soon-to-be "mother-in-law" is hosting an engagement party on New Year's Eve. You have four days to sober up and pull yourself together."

"Damn you all!"

"I love you, too, Seb. And I suggest you be on your best behavior. The Ashby family is very upset with you. You have a lot of people to appease."

"Shit."

"Especially the sisters."

"Why especially?" Sebastian snapped.

"Well, the Ashby sisters were always dead set against you marrying Henrietta. Once they suspected you might be smitten with the girl, they were determined to tear the two of you apart."

Sebastian hissed, "Is that why her sisters were always fussing about?"

Peter nodded. "They wanted to make sure you never had a moment alone with Henry; that you never had a chance to disgrace the girl. Well, so much for that." Peter adjusted his top hat. "And then there's the baron."

"What about the baron?"

"He's quite miffed that you're stealing his 'darling boy' away?"

Sebastian rubbed his tired brow.

"And then you have Lady Ashby to confront."

"Surely *she's* happy about the wedding. She's been hosting masquerades for years hoping to marrying off Henrietta. Isn't she getting her wish?"

"Yes, but she could have done without the scandal."

Sebastian gnashed his teeth. "I'm *not* the one who caused the scandal."

"A trifling detail." Peter headed for the door. "The engagement party is in four days, remember, so clean yourself up and be prepared to pacify a lot of angry Ashbys."

Angry Ashbys? *He* should be the angry one. *He* was the one being carted down the aisle in bloody chains.

"Buck up, Seb." Peter opened the door. "Think of it this way: it's a new start to a new year."

Peter left the room and closed the door behind him.

Sebastian, still dizzy, stretched out on the bed. He closed his eyes, willing the thrumming pain into submission.

Marriage.

To Henrietta.

The fog in his head made it hard for the words to sink into his brain. And how had the letter made its way around Town anyway?

He tried to think back … but his memories were awash in shadows and sounds and distorted faces. He remembered reading the letter, but then …

"Shit."

Sebastian stuffed his head under the pillow, for he had not the strength to get up and draw the drapes. He couldn't remember what had happened to the blasted letter after he'd read it. He didn't want to think about the cursed piece of paper anymore. He didn't want to think about the approaching wedding, either. Or his intended bride. He wanted to sleep and forget about the nightmare his life had just become.

But something pinched his pinky finger.

Sebastian stuck his head out from under the pillow and squinted. The ring on his finger felt tight, his knuckles swollen. He must have gotten into some sort of row the other night; he couldn't remember. But it was the design on the ring that really captivated him. The interwoven rope, the knot.

He thought back to Christmas Eve, the night Henrietta had given him the ring as a gift. He remembered the enchanting look in her eyes, the spirited sound of her laughter. He remembered the scent of jasmine in her hair … and that kiss under the mistletoe.

Something twitched in his belly at the sensual memory. And now the vixen was going to become his wife.

The door opened.

The housekeeper, Mrs. Molony, shuffled inside. Without so much as a "good morning," the stout woman set right to work on making the bed—around his body. She was so accustomed to his frequent binges that she did her domestic duty without complaint or hesitation.

Humming an Irish jig as she fluffed the pillows around his head, she suddenly paused.

"When did you start believing in Irish folklore, m'lord?"

"What the deuce are you talking about, Mrs. Molony?"

"The ring." She pointed to the bauble on his finger. "It's a Celtic love knot."

Sebastian eyed the ring again. "It is?"

"Aye." Mrs. Molony moved about the room. She gathered the vest, the coat crumpled on the floor. "According to Irish lore, he who wears the charm will attract his one true love." The housekeeper lifted a curious gray brow. "And who might you be trying to attract, m'lord?"

But she didn't really want an answer. Having had the pleasure of ruffling his surly feathers, she gathered the laundry and was out the door.

Sebastian glared at the shiny ring on his finger. Henrietta, the devious chit! She had given him a Celtic love knot.

He should not be surprised by her trickery. She was a skilled seductress. And she was going to be his wife. He was going to have to live with her feminine wiles for the rest of his days. He should be outraged. A part of him was. But another part of him was not so incensed. Marriage did afford him *one* pleasure.

Buck up? Oh, Sebastian intended to do that very thing. He intended to enjoy Henrietta very much—in his bed.

CHAPTER 19

Henrietta glanced at the grandfather clock. It was almost midnight—and Ravenswood had yet to arrive.

The villain! He was probably at his vile club, too busy fornicating with a "nun" to come to his own engagement party.

Her heart cramped as she imagined him in the catacombs, wallowing in debauchery, touching another woman … the way he had touched her that night in the library.

Henrietta quickly dismissed the disturbing vision from her mind. She didn't care if Ravenswood touched another woman. Good riddance! He would never touch her again, that was for certain.

But did the man have to humiliate her in front of the *ton*? Was he really so angry about getting married? It's not like she was delighted about the wedding, didn't he know? He didn't need to make the evening more intolerable for her by deserting her … unless he enjoyed making her suffer.

Her heart fluttered at the grim thought. To think she had ever cared for the scoundrel. That she had once believed he cared for her. Secretly *loved* her, even!

She bit her bottom lip to keep it from trembling. Rotten tears! How could she still cry for the blackguard?

"Henry, my boy, are you unwell?"

Henrietta glanced at her father and smiled. It was a rather shaky smile, but still, she was glad to see him. He had spent the last few days in seclusion, and it had taken quite a bit of coaxing to get him out of the doldrums.

"I'm fine, Papa. It's a little too warm in here, I think."

"Quite. Quite. Too warm." The baron locked his hands behind his back. "You and I shall play a game of billiards, Henry. How does that sound? We'll get away from all this ruckus?"

"Thank you, Papa, but I think we must stay and host the celebration."

However wretched it might be, she thought. An engagement party without the groom? The society papers would be awash with speculation. But Henrietta wasn't going to cower and dash off to play billiards. She was going to stand there with a fixed smile, and brave the curious looks and whispered words. She wasn't going to dishonor her family even more by disappearing in a scandalous fashion.

The baron made a sour face. "It's a curious night, Henry. Indeed it is. Ravenswood isn't here to enjoy the festivities. You don't want to play billiards." He sighed. "It's all so peculiar."

"Nicholas, get away from the girl!"

The baroness was approaching, her deportment stern.

"Nicholas, shoo!" Lady Ashby flicked her wrist. "You look cross. Don't scold the girl in public."

"What rubbish!" The baron snorted. "Why, I was just having a friendly chat with the boy."

"Well, the guests are beginning to think you're unhappy about the approaching wedding."

"I *am* unhappy, Lara." The baron huffed. "The boy's too young to be leg-shackled. Nasty business, I say. Nasty."

"Yes, nasty business." Lady Ashby offered her youngest daughter a pointed look. "But the girl's made her choice, Nicholas."

Henrietta winced. Her mother was referring to the letter she had written to Sebastian. A sensual letter of apology that the *ton* believed was part of a lover's quarrel. But since Ravenswood wasn't at the party, the blasted man, the *ton* was beginning to suspect it all a matter of unrequited love, that Henrietta had dreamed up the affair in her head. And since she *had* dreamed up the affair in her head, it was all the more embarrassing.

"Come along, Nicholas." The baroness tugged at his arm. "We have guests to greet." Lady Ashby whispered to Henrietta, "And you, my dear, had best get back to smiling."

The baron looked over his shoulder. "Billiards, Henry. Billiards!"

Henrietta watched her parents disappear into the crush, then sighed.

"Have you forgiven me yet, Henry?"

She pinched her lips.

"I didn't think so," said Peter, holding two glasses of chilled champagne. He offered her one, which she accepted. "Please understand, Henry, I wanted what was best for both of you. You cared so much for Sebastian, and I was so sure that he cared for you."

Her heart throbbed at his words. She, too, had believed that very thing. She was such a dunce!

"I made a mistake, Henry. I should have told you about Sebastian's 'habits' from the start. Will you forgive me?"

She sniffed. "Yes, Peter, I will."

There was no sense being mad at Peter anyway. It was her own wretched fault for being such a ninny.

"A toast." Peter lifted the flute. "To new beginnings."

They clinked glasses.

"And it's getting off to a charming start," she said dryly. "It's almost midnight, Peter, and he still isn't here."

Peter glanced at the grandfather clock. "So it is." He looked back at her. "But he *will* be here, Henry. Trust me."

"And how can you be so sure of that?"

"Because I have to believe there is a little good inside my brother."

Henrietta could admire his familial devotion. But she didn't have to believe in it herself. "You have more faith in your brother than I do."

"Yes, I suppose that is my failing." He smiled. "Would you care to dance?"

"Thank you, Peter, but no. Why don't you dance with your wife? Penelope looks like she needs a respite from all the pestering guests."

They both glanced across the room to see Penelope fending off a gaggle of matrons, peppering her with questions about the viscount's absence. "He had a pressing matter of business," she deflected. "He'll be here as soon as time permits." Poor Penelope.

Peter offered her a tender smile. "Will you be all right, Henry?"

"Yes, I will. Now off with you, Peter. Go and rescue your wife."

Peter nodded and set off.

Henrietta watched as Peter and Penelope waltzed in the anteroom. How odd to see one brother so content, so at ease with his wife, so happy, even. And to know that the other brother was so dark in spirit? It was all so peculiar, as Papa would say. How had Sebastian drifted so far into the shadows of life?

"Good evening, Miss Ashby."

Henrietta looked up at the handsome young man, and returned his smile. "Good evening, my lord."

"Emerson, please. I have come in place of my father, the Earl of Ormsby."

Henrietta had heard the name before, but she had never met the earl or his son. Was Mama inviting strangers to the party? It wouldn't surprise her. The woman was determined to make a good show of the engagement bash; make *it* the talk of the *ton* and not the scandalous letter Henrietta had penned to Sebastian.

"Is your father unwell, Lord Emerson?"

"He loathes the cold, I'm afraid. Might I congratulate you on his behalf?"

"Yes, of course. Thank you, my lord."

Henrietta tried to sound like a cheery bride, but it was a deuced bother, the façade. She had to go along with the charade, though. She had to sweep up the mess she'd made with that damned letter.

"It is a splendid match, Miss Ashby." The young lord's smile quivered. "If I might be so bold, Ravenswood is a very fortunate man."

There was something familiar about Lord Emerson. As his smile cracked, it triggered a memory of … well, she wasn't quite sure, but she suddenly didn't care for the man's attention. What was it about him? His eyes?

Henrietta furrowed her brow. "Lord Emerson, have we met before?"

"It is possible, Miss Ashby. We move in very similar circles."

"I distinctly remember you from somewhere."

"Perhaps I remind you of someone?"

Henrietta wasn't satisfied with that explanation. "There is something familiar about you."

"Such as?"

"Your eyes."

He lifted a brow. "My eyes, Miss Ashby?"

"Something about the color … purple feathers!"

Emerson started. "Pardon, Miss Ashby?"

"Purple feathers. I remember now. You had a mask of purple feathers. We must have met at a masquerade ball. Last summer, I believe."

"You are right, Miss Ashby." He smiled. "The masquerade. I do remember now that you mention it."

There, she had solved that mystery. And now she could get on with her assessment of Emerson. He had good family connections. He was articulate. He was a handsome fellow, albeit dull. But he was pleasant. He was the sort of man she *should* have set her cap for all those years ago. Not the dashing rogue Ravenswood.

"When is the happy union, Miss Ashby?"

"On Twelfth Night." One long and dreadful week away. "We will be married at the chapel in town."

"I cannot wait to attend, Miss Ashby."

How distressing that the guests were more eager about the wedding than the bride!

"Yes, I'm looking forward to it myself."

Lud, she sounded so insipid!

"Well, Miss Ashby, until the joyous day, I bid you good evening."

Emerson bowed and retreated into the crowd.

Just then the grandfather clock struck the hour of twelve.

Midnight! And Ravenswood was *still* absent.

Henrietta downed the rest of her champagne. She'd had enough. She was going to bed.

Three. Four. Five chimes.

She skirted across the room. She had made a good show of it. But her betrothed was still detained by "business." There was no sense in her standing there anymore, under the scrutiny of the guests. She was utterly fagged.

Ten. Eleven. Twelve chimes.

It was after midnight.

The assembly room door opened.

Henrietta gasped. "Ravenswood!"

He looked like a fallen angel, dark, yet still sinfully beautiful. And those eyes! The deepest shade of blue—and so full of intent.

Sebastian headed straight for her.

Henrietta clutched her belly. He had come, the blackguard. And dressed in the most striking attire. Dark breeches and boots. Form fitted coat, tailed. A sharp blue waistcoat, so snug against his strapping chest.

The flutters of her heart quickened even more. For four days she had cried and cursed his black heart, so determined to loathe him. And now here he was, a formidable rogue. And she could not utter a word of resentment. Oh, it was there in her gut, the fury. But she was having a deuced hard time voicing her dander aloud.

"Happy New Year, Henry."

He whispered the words.

Her toes curled.

And then he kissed her soundly.

CHAPTER 20

The sweet taste of champagne on Henrietta's warm lips had a besotting effect on Sebastian. Not the buzz from the guests, nor the music in the anteroom distracted him from the kiss—only the sharp cut of her teeth was rather jarring.

He let her go and licked his lips, tasting blood. She had snatched away his bachelorhood by writing that scandalous letter, and now she had the brass to bite him?

"Is that any way to greet your fiancé?"

"Why did you kiss me?" she hissed.

"It's New Year's Eve? Isn't it the way I'm supposed to greet you?"

Henrietta lifted her darling chin, took in a deep breath, and said quietly, "Go to blazes."

Sebastian quirked a mordant grin.

The feisty little hoyden. He was going to enjoy bedding her. Her rebellious eyes and defiant spirit already aroused him.

"You look bewitching tonight," he whispered, eyes dropping to the sweeping cut of her fashionable frock. "Red suits your passionate nature."

"And black suits your dark and twisted heart."

"Touché, Henry."

"My name is Miss Ashby."

How formal. Cold and haughty, too. She had pestered him for years to call her by her nickname, and now she preferred their former, proper rapport? Very well, he would play along—at least until he got the fiery chit into bed.

"I apologize, Miss Ashby."

"Rot!' she snapped. "You're late."

"Am I?" He glanced at the clock. "So I am. How dreadful. I hope I didn't cause too much of a stir."

The deep swell of her lush breasts was hard to miss. She was trying to keep a cap on her temper. Had he ruffled her feathers with his tardiness? Capital. He was determined to wrest back some control of his miserable life. And since he could not choose his bride, he was damned well going to choose what time he showed up for his engagement party.

"Where have you been?" she gritted. "That vile club of yours?"

He lifted a brow. "Jealous, Miss Ashby?"

"What rot!"

He had never liked her possessive tendencies before, but now … now he wasn't quite so averse to them. She had to care for him—even a little—to be jealous. And he liked the thought of that, as well.

"I rather think you're jealous," Sebastian murmured with a wolfish smile.

"I rather think you're a scoundrel."

"I am, Miss Ashby." He lifted his hand to thumb the smooth texture of her rosy cheek. "And you are jealous."

"I loathe you."

She shivered under his touch, indicating otherwise, warming his blood. He had prepared himself for her contempt. But now to feel the quiver of her arousal did his roguish heart much good.

"I'm flattered, Miss Ashby."

"I'm tired." Henrietta turned her cheek away. "I'm going to bed."

"Would you like me to join you?"

She gasped. "Why, you rotten—"

"Something the matter, Miss Ashby?" He slipped his arm around her waist and caressed the low curve of her back, insensible to the spectacle he was making in front of the guests. "You and I are about to be married. And since you've welcomed me into your bed before …"

"I will *never* welcome you into my bed again."

"Is that so?" he drawled, unconvinced.

"Our marriage will be in name only. I will never let you touch me, Ravenswood—ever!"

Sebastian frowned. He delved deep into her bay brown eyes, searching for truth. And he realized the chit was serious!

Now he was *really* livid.

"What about an heir, Miss Ashby?"

"Peter's will do just fine." She bumped his hand off her midriff. "You've always said so yourself."

The muscles in his jaw and neck stiffened. "And if Peter doesn't have an heir?"

She looked perplexed, like she hadn't thought about that possibility. But she quickly gathered her features. "Why don't we wait and see what happens in the next, oh, five years? If there's no heir by then, we'll discuss the matter again."

Five *years*! Did she think to keep him from her room—her bed—for that long? Even the whole of their marriage?

Like hell! It was already insufferable, being forced to wed. But he damn well wasn't going to marry a cold fish!

He'd already had a carnal taste of Henrietta. She was a feisty little wanton in bed. It was the only perk to the whole miserable affair. And if she thought to deny him her charming curves, her plump breasts … well, Sebastian wasn't going to stand for it.

"Good evening, Ravenswood."

Sebastian smoothed his rankled features into a bland smile. "Good evening, Lord Ashby."

The baron stretched out his hand in greeting. "How are your business affairs, Ravenswood?"

Sebastian accepted the offered hand and wrinkled his brow. "My business affairs?"

"The reason you were detained, my lord," said Henrietta.

"Ah, yes, my business affairs. All in good order, Lord Ashby."

"Glad to hear it, Ravenswood. Glad to hear it."

The baron was stiff and formal and so unlike his usual cheerful self. Well, Peter had warned him the baron was cantankerous. After all, Sebastian was stealing away the man's "darling boy."

"Baron Ashby, I understand you have leather tip cue sticks?"

Henrietta offered him a quizzical look.

"Why, yes, Ravenswood," said the baron. "Yes, I do."

"We must play a game of billiards, my lord."

The baron's eyes brightened. "What a capital idea, Ravenswood!"

"Splendid!" Sebastian smiled. "How about a game tonight?"

The baron beamed. "A game? Tonight? Why, yes, Ravenswood. I would be delighted."

Henrietta pinched her lips and crossed her arms under her breasts. The baron was an easy man to cajole. She might not appreciate that, but Sebastian did. He had other, more pressing matters to attend to, and the sooner he appeased every angry Ashby at the party, the sooner he could upbraid his betrothed for even suggesting he steer clear of her bed.

And speaking of every angry Ashby …

"Good evening, Lady Ashby."

The baroness came to stand beside her husband. She, too, was stiff and cold, and she offered him a cutting glance.

"Good evening, my lord."

"You look lovely tonight."

"Thank you, my lord," she said crisply.

"I have a favor to ask of you, Lady Ashby."

The baroness opened her fan with a snap. "Yes, Ravenswood?"

"You must take my place at the Royal Pavilion in Brighton."

Lady Ashby's fan flickered fast. "The Royal Pavilion, my lord?"

"It's in a month's time. I've been invited to an assembly by the King himself. And you are family, Lady Ashby, so I insist you take my place. I shall be engaged elsewhere, I'm afraid." *Bedding my wife.* "I must beg you to go in my stead."

Her lips twisting into a smile, the baroness—so besotted with pomp and presentation—quickly replied, "Why, I'd be honored, Ravenswood."

"Splendid!"

Sebastian knew for a fact the baroness had never been invited to one of the royal assemblies. She had lamented about the slight for years. Surely she would never be cross with him again for orchestrating the invitation.

The baroness beamed at her husband and took him by the arm. "Come, Nicholas. We have guests to entertain." She nodded to Sebastian. "Lord Ravenswood."

Sebastian bowed. "Lady Ashby."

The baroness dragged her husband away.

The baron whispered in flight, "Billiards later, Ravenswood!"

That was two Ashbys thoroughly stroked, flattered and appeased. Now he need only placate the sisters …

Aha! He'd have the finest lace and ribbon and fringe in all of France delivered to their door. That should exonerate him nicely.

Now to throttle his betrothed.

Sebastian slipped a firm arm around Henrietta's waist and steered her to a more private nook. "We have a matter of business to discuss, Miss Ashby."

She smacked his hand away. "We have nothing to discuss, my lord. I will not be so easily mollified. You cannot offer to play billiards with me or drag me off to Brighton to dance with the King, and expect me to forgive you."

"Forgive *me*?" he choked. "For what?"

"You bandied that letter all over London and ruined me!"

He growled, "I did *not* bandy that letter. And might I remind you, *I*, too, was ruined by the scandal."

"How dreadful for you." She smirked, then: "But if you didn't show the letter all over Town, then who did?"

"I have no idea, but I can assure you, Miss Ashby, I will throttle the culprit as soon as I find him."

"Or her, my lord. You do have so many lovely 'nuns' in your life. Women can be so devious, my lord."

Devious indeed. Imagine trapping a man into marriage, then denying him the marriage bed. It was a bloody sin!

"Let's not forget who wrote that letter in the first place," he growled.

"Oh, I won't forget. And I will pay for my folly all the rest of my days—with my marriage to you!"

She flounced off. A bit shaky in her step, but still, she had made her feelings perfectly clear—she hated him!

"Evening, Seb."

"Go to hell, Peter."

Peter was positively tickled.

Sebastian looked beyond his brother's annoying head to see a gaggle of protective sisters surround Henrietta. How was he supposed to get close to his betrothed with all those harridans buzzing about?

He sighed. "I've come to marry her, Peter."

Peter rocked on his heels, gleeful. "'Course you have."

"But it looks like she loathes me."

"'Course she does."

"So you, brother, are going to help me win her back."

"'Course I will."

"You'll take care of the sisters?"

"Already on it."

Peter strutted off, a light spring to his step.

Sebastian glared at the sexy hoyden from across the room, waiting for the ideal opportunity to be alone with her.

The nerve of the chit to deny him—her soon-to-be husband—that deliciously tempting body of hers. Well, there was only one thing left to do. He was going to have to seduce the willful Miss Ashby.

CHAPTER 21

Henrietta stood on the terrace edge, gazing at the stars. She didn't have a wrap. She'd been far too eager to get away from the festivities—and Ravenswood's smoldering kiss—to fetch one.

Alone, for her sisters had been summoned to the nursery—the children were in an uproar of some sorts—Henrietta let the chill of winter nip at her nose. Maybe it would nip at her heart, too, and cap the teeming emotions in her breast.

That dastardly knave! Ravenswood had strolled into the parlor at the stroke of midnight, tried to charm his way into *her* bed, and then had the gall to look stricken at the thought of being denied his marital right.

She humphed. Was she supposed to ignore his foul behavior? Pretend he wasn't a degenerate? He had smashed her heart to bits that night at the abbey. She didn't trust the man. She didn't even *like* the man anymore. And she would not let him near her heart or her body again. She'd pelt him with rocks first.

However, there was one misfortune she had not anticipated: the lack of an heir. In her steely determination to be rid of Ravenswood's touch, she'd forgotten about a babe. If she barred the viscount from her bed, she would never be a mother.

There was a sharp pang in her chest at the thought of being childless. She knew firsthand the grief it caused her sister Penelope. But Henrietta quickly dismissed the ache. It was better for her to remain fruitless. Peter and Penelope might still have an heir to secure the estate. Henrietta need not bring an innocent babe into Ravenswood's sinful world. The viscount would make a terrible father, teach their child to indulge in vice. And she could not bear to witness the degeneration of her own son, the corruption of her own daughter.

Henrietta bristled. A warm coat slipped over her shoulders, the scent of Eau de Cologne stirring her senses.

She needed rocks!

"You'll catch a chill, Miss Ashby."

Oh, that gruff male voice! Did it have to make her quiver so?

She didn't dare turn around. "I'm not cold."

"You're shivering, Miss Ashby."

Sebastian rubbed her shoulders in slow and sensual caresses, warming her blood. Did he think to beguile her with his gallantry? Henrietta had more fight in her than that.

"What are you doing here, Ravenswood?"

"Can't I visit with my fiancée?"

Oh, now he wanted to spend time with her? It had suited him just fine, deserting her for most of the engagement party, but now he was ready to cavort with her? Did he want more kisses?

That did it. Henrietta whirled around.

Big mistake. One look at the sinfully striking viscount, and her breath hitched. Her heart pattered, too. And that all too familiar sensation—desire—heated her belly. She might not like the rogue, but she still found him tempting to look at. Madam Jacqueline had warned her about such a polar sentiment. She hadn't believed the woman—until now.

"Won't it ruin your roguish reputation, visiting with your intended bride?"

"It will ruin my roguish reputation even more if my own bride despises me." Then in a low voice: "Come, Miss Ashby, let us forget about the past."

She was strapped for words. The gall of the man to suggest she overlook his wickedness. The bounder had broken her heart! How was she supposed to forget *that*?

"You and I are to be married, Miss Ashby. Let us begin anew." He stuck out his hand. "Friends?"

She gawked at the offered truce. Was the cold seeping into the man's brain, freezing all his good sense? "You and I are not friends, Ravenswood."

"Why, Miss Ashby? Because we had a tiff?"

Tiff?

"Friends do quarrel, you know?" he said. "And a good friend will always forgive another's transgression."

"Then I must not be a very good friend," she said tightly.

He tsked. "Don't say that, Miss Ashby. You are a very dear friend … and a soon-to-be wife."

"Well, then, as your soon-to-be-wife, why don't you answer the question I asked you back inside the house?"

"And what question would that be?"

"Why are you so late?"

"Ah, so you're still jealous." Then softly: "I rather like it when you're jealous, Miss Ashby."

"I am *not* jealous. I just want to know the reason for your delay."

"Well, it is winter, Miss Ashby. The roads are terrible."

She humphed. "I don't believe you. Every other guest arrived on time."

"Bravo for every other guest."

Oh, the maddening man! "You left me alone on purpose, admit it."

"And why would I do that, Miss Ashby?"

"To humiliate me, you blackguard!"

He tsked again. "Such language, Miss Ashby."

He dared to lecture her on polite behavior? A lecher of the highest order? She was desperate for a rock.

"You were at the Hellfire Club, weren't you?" she charged. "Dallying with a *nun*!"

"And what if I was?"

She gasped. "You admit it?"

"I admit nothing, Miss Ashby. I only ask: what *if* I was there? Would you be jealous?"

"Rot! I don't care if you romp around with a skirt."

"Is that so?" he drawled.

She gathered her shaky breath. All right, perhaps she cared a little. But not in the way he was suggesting. Jealousy, her foot! She was thinking about her respectability, that's all. The respectability of her family. She didn't want the Ashby name disgraced by Ravenswood's wild behavior.

She huffed, "I expect you to be discrete about your affairs."

"Well, I wasn't planning to have any affairs, but if you insist ..."

She gnashed her teeth. "If you have even a dash of honor in your soul, you will not disgrace me—a *friend*—in public."

"Miss Ashby, I would never do anything so shameful." He brushed his thumb across the ridge of her brow in a feathery stroke. "Would it please you to hear I was not at the abbey?" He traced the pad of his thumb across her frosty cheek, down the rigid length of her jaw. "Would it please you to hear I haven't been back to the abbey since the night we quarreled?"

She shivered under his oh-so-ginger touch. Breathless, she said, "I don't believe you."

"Oh, believe me, Miss Ashby. For the past four days I've been shut up in my room, thinking about you—and our pending nuptial."

It took her lips a few moments to catch up with her bewildering thoughts. Was the daft man talking about the wedding night? As if she would ever consider letting him near her in *that* way again.

"A pity you squandered away your nights daydreaming," she quipped.

"Do not pity me, Miss Ashby. My time was pleasantly engaged with thoughts of you."

Oh, damn her treacherous heart for pulsing so fast!

"I'm privy to your charms, Ravenswood. You will not win your way back into my bed with a few whispered words and an artful touch."

He reared his head—and hand—back, aghast. "Why, Miss Ashby, is *that* what you think of me? I'm hurt, truly I am. I was only thinking about our marital life together." He lifted his eyes heavenward, as though deep in thought. "I suppose I will have to buy a house in the more fashionable part of London, give up my bachelor residence for good. And you shall want to decorate the dwelling I'm sure, so I'll summon an interior designer post haste." His smoldering eyes met hers once more. "But I've no intention of bedding you, I assure you."

"Oh."

Why did her heart hurt? She had no desire to carouse with the viscount, even if he should woo her. He was a villain, remember? A fiend. Good riddance!

"You've made your feelings perfectly clear, Miss Ashby. Our marriage is to be in name only. I respect your decision."

Henrietta eyed him, unconvinced. "You do?"

A curt nod. "Of course, I do. I'm not a devil through and through, you know? I do have a 'dash' of honor." A dark fire sparked in his eyes. "And I shall prove it to you. We will settle this matter once and for all."

"Settle what matter?"

"Our strife, of course."

"And how do you propose we do that?"

"We shall have a contest."

"Gamble, you mean?"

He nodded. "It is the only reasonable way for two members of the peerage to settle a dispute. If I win, we start anew. Wipe the slate clean, if you will. And as forfeit, I can ask anything of you I wish."

Henrietta took in a sharp breath. *He* would request another kiss, she was sure. Or some other sexual favor, scoundrel that he was.

"And if I win?" she asked.

"Then I suppose we don't begin anew, and as forfeit you can ask anything of me in return."

"A house, for instance?"

"Yes, I already mentioned—"

"No, I mean a house of my own, where *you* cannot visit." She smiled at the thought. "And you can keep your bachelor residence to boot."

Now *that* was the perfect way to spend the rest of her married days with Ravenswood—apart.

There was a dark kindle in the viscount's eyes. He was quiet for a moment. She doubted he would accept her terms. But at length, he nodded.

"Very well, Miss Ashby. A house it is."

She scrunched her face in misgiving. He was much too cavalier for her liking. What was the man scheming?

"I think I'd rather face you on the dueling field, Ravenswood."

"Miss Ashby, you are a woman, whatever your father might say."

"I'm also a good shot. It would be a fair fight."

"You would shoot me?" The fire in his eyes burned bright. "You hate me that much?"

She stared at his mesmerizing eyes, forgot her words for a moment, then said, "Shoot you, yes. Kill you, no."

But she'd like to wound the blackguard, make him feel some of the pain he'd made her feel.

"Well, Miss Ashby, while you might be able to shoot me, I could never shoot you."

She huffed. He was playing the gallant knight again. But she'd indulge his peculiar request. Anything to be rid of the man. She trusted even a knave like Ravenswood would honor a challenge loss. And if she won the wager, she intended to buy the biggest house she could find and bankrupt him furnishing it.

"A contest it is then," she said.

"Wise decision, Miss Ashby."

What decision? It's not like she had a choice in the matter.

"What shall we wager?" she wondered. "Who can annoy the other the most?"

"Touché, Miss Ashby." He even offered her a little smile that made her heart jump. "I was thinking more along the lines of a duel—with snow."

"Snow?"

Sebastian hunched down and gathered a lump of snow into his hands. "Do you see that statue?"

Henrietta cast her eyes over the garden. "The marble cherubs holding a bird bath?"

"That's right." He squashed the snow into a hard ball. "Whoever hits a cherub wins the duel."

Henrietta eyed the statue. About thirty paces, she reckoned. She could do it. "Very well, then."

She tucked her arms into Sebastian's coat, to keep the garment in place, then she, too, hunched and collected the fresh fallen snow. Rolling it in her hands, she watched her opponent.

Sebastian was first. He took a step forward, brought his arm back, paused, then pitched the snowball across the garden.

It skimmed a cherub's arm.

Sebastian didn't look too happy about his flimsy shot.

Henrietta, on the other hand, was tickled.

"I think I can beat that," she said with a smug air, and flounced over to the spot opposite the statue.

Sebastian took a step back.

But she could feel his hot stare on her the entire time. Well, he would not intimidate her. In just a moment she was going to be rid of the man for good.

Henrietta eyed a cherub. She was a skilled marksman with a gun or arrow. Papa had made sure to teach her—well, he had hired someone to teach her the skill. Papa didn't have very good aim himself. But Henrietta was a brilliant shot. Always had been. This should be as easy as pinching pastries from the cook's pantry.

She swung her arm, let the snowball fly ... and watched it miss the statue entirely.

Henrietta stared, dumbfounded.

She had lost.

How had she lost?

A triumphant smile slowly curled the viscount's lips. "Well, Miss Ashby, it looks like you've lost."

She gnashed her teeth. "So it would seem."

"That means I am the winner."

The conceited blackguard! "Yes, Ravenswood, I know."

"And I can ask anything of you I wish."

She huffed. "So ask."

He took a step back and made a sweeping bow. "Will you do me the honor of a dance?"

What, no kisses?

He held out his hand. "Shall we?"

Henrietta stared at his hand, tickles of warmth spreading throughout her body. She was being a deuced ninny about this. She had lost the wager. Fair was fair. She needn't be squeamish. She just had to dance with the bounder and be done with it. She would find some other way to oust the knave from her life. There was no sense idling. She would not let the viscount intimidate her. She had more valor than that.

Henrietta slipped her hand in his, shivering at his touch. The music from the anteroom seeped outside, soft waves of sound intruding on the quiet terrace.

"You and I have never dance before?" He gathered her in his arms for a waltz. "Why is that?"

Henrietta gritted, "Because you've never asked me to dance."

"Ah, yes." He swept her across the terrace. "But we were not betrothed back then. We are now, though, and I think this is a splendid way to begin anew, don't you?"

She didn't say anything. He was arousing feelings inside her: feelings of warmth and security, even. Since girlhood she had known she would feel safe in the viscount's arms. That the rogue could still inspire her foolish childhood fancy was intolerable. She wanted to dash back inside the house; to barricade herself from the viscount's wicked charms.

"It's starting to snow," he said softly.

Henrietta lifted her gaze as snow drifted from the night sky. She whirled beneath the falling puffs; a horrendous sorrow washing over her. It was so perfect, she thought. The romantic night, the handsome viscount in her arms—and it was all an illusion.

"What's the matter, Miss Ashby?"

He whispered the words. Henrietta almost wished he'd said the name Henry, instead.

"I'm feeling dizzy," she fibbed. She wanted out of the viscount's arms. She wanted out of the illusion.

Sebastian stopped. "I'll escort you back inside the house."

"No." She shrugged off his coat and handed him the garment. "I'll return to the house alone. I think I will retire to bed. You have a game of billiards to play with Papa."

She headed for the terrace doors.

"Goodnight, Miss Ashby," he said quietly after her.

Henrietta paused, then quickly skirted back inside the house.

~ * ~

A figure lurked in the shadows.

Emerson was in hiding from Ravenswood. He did not want an encore of their last row, so humiliating for him. He had come to tonight's festivity to rejoice in his machinations, to see the viscount wallow in agony ... but something had gone awry.

It was obvious the little slut didn't want the viscount anymore. But the viscount so earnestly wanted her.

Peculiar.

His diabolic mind whirling, Emerson started to think it might work out even better this way. If the hussy Miss Ashby resented the viscount, it would make the lovelorn Ravenswood miserable. All Emerson had to do was keep the girl at odds with the viscount, make sure she crushed the ogre's heart to bits. Disgraced him, even.

Now *that* was an even better form of revenge.

CHAPTER 22

A little bell chimed as Sebastian opened the door. He stepped inside the shop and perused the shelves of knickknacks: porcelain dolls, ceramic vases, China figurines. He just might find a treasure of some sort in here, he mused. He had already been to three other establishments, but had failed to find the right gift for Henrietta.

Last night's seduction had not gone so well as he had hoped. For a man accustomed to getting what he wanted from a woman, that was very discouraging. At one point during last night's waltz, Henrietta had looked positively green!

It was time to amend his approach to courting. The chit was smitten with him. But she was fighting her attraction to him. He needed something with which to soften her ornery disposition. And a gift should redeem him nicely. It had always worked for him in the past. After a row with a mistress, he'd flash a pricey trinket and all her tears would magically disappear.

Behind the ornate wood counter was an elderly gentleman. "Good morning, my lord." He smiled. "How may I help you?"

Sebastian eyed the trinkets along the wall. "I'm looking for something special."

"For your wife, my lord?"

A tight knot formed in the viscount's belly. Yes, Henrietta was going to be his wife. But it was a brutal business, getting used to the word.

"My soon-to-be wife," said Sebastian.

With a sage nod, the elderly shopkeeper moved away from the counter and headed for a cluttered shelf. He picked up a shiny box with opal inlays.

"How about this, my lord?"

The shopkeeper opened the box and turned the tiny key.

A quaint tune escaped. Charming. But not charming enough. He was looking for a unique present, one with veiled implications mayhap. The chit had given him such a gift on Christmas Eve: a ring with a Celtic love knot. Now he had to find something equally significant with which to woo his stubborn Henrietta.

"What else do you have?" said Sebastian.

Beside the window was a table filled with trinkets. The shopkeeper lifted a small clock with hand painted daisies.

Sebastian eyed the piece. Pretty. But Henrietta was never on time for anything. She might think such a gift an ill-mannered gesture on his part.

The viscount shook his head. "Anything else?"

As the shopkeeper shuffled about, a reflection caught Sebastian's eye. "What is that?"

"My lord?"

"Over there." He pointed across the crowded room. "Inside the glass display."

The shopkeeper pushed a gold birdcage aside to reach the display. He opened the case and removed the trinket. "This, my lord?"

"Yes, that's it." A slow smile spread across the viscount's face. "It's perfect."

~ * ~

"Ouch!" cried Henrietta at the sharp pain in her arse.

"Forgive me, miss," said the seamstress.

"Stand still, Henry," the baroness reproached. "There's just a few more pins."

Henrietta sighed. One more fitting and then she wouldn't have to think about the wedding dress anymore. All the wedding arrangements were making her harebrained. It was a faithful reminder of her disgraceful betrothal to Ravenswood. She needed a breath, a moment of repose from all the preparations.

"*Ouch!*"

"Forgive me, miss," burbled the seamstress, pins trapped between her teeth.

"Stop squirming, Henry," from the baroness. "Whatever is the matter with you?"

The seamstress plucked one last pin from between her teeth and jabbed it into the back of Henrietta's dress. "Finished, miss."

Well, thank heavens for that! Henrietta's poor rump was bruised, no doubt.

"Now be careful, Henry." The baroness offered her hand for support. "Don't tear the lace."

Henrietta took her mother's outstretched hand and stepped off the stool. The seamstress unfastened the buttons, and gingerly, Henrietta slipped out of the pink satin and fine lace garment.

In a few minutes, she was draped in a sage green day dress and scurrying from the room, leaving Mama and the seamstress to quibble over stitching details.

But the rest of the house was full of activity, too. There was so much to do before Twelfth Night. Flowers to arrange. Cakes to bake. Linens to iron. Silverware to polish. Thankfully her sisters and Mama insisted on helping with the preparations.

Henrietta moved through the house, searching for Papa. Perhaps he'd like to play a game of billiards now? She hoped so. She needed a respite.

Henrietta tiptoed through the passageways so as not to attract the viscount's attention, for he, too, was sheltered somewhere in the house, the dratted man. The family had insisted Ravenswood stay at the house until the day of the ceremony. Despite all his charm, it seemed no one trusted the rogue to show up for the wedding. The arrangement had put Henrietta in high dungeon. But ironically, it had pleased the viscount.

Odd. The man was acting so peculiar, spouting fresh starts and clean slates. It wasn't like Ravenswood at all. And it made her wonder all the more what the viscount was scheming. She certainly didn't believe he had transformed into a gentleman, that he respected her decision to marry in name alone. The rogue was up to something. But what?

"Sneaking about, Miss Ashby?"

She had not been quiet enough, it seemed.

Henrietta squared her shoulders and turned around to confront the viscount, prepared with a retort. But one look at the dashing man and all thoughts of a rejoinder deserted her.

He had a mischievous look in his eyes. More of an imp than a fiend. He was smiling, too. And she didn't like the fact that his devastating smile still curled her toes. It made it deuced hard to hate the man.

"I'm not sneaking about," she said firmly. "I'm looking for Papa."

"The baron is in his study."

A curt bob of the head. "Thank you." And she pivoted, heading for the study.

"But he is asleep, Miss Ashby."

Henrietta stilled.

"I was just there myself," he said. "The baron is napping, I'm afraid."

Drat.

"Perhaps I can assist you, Miss Ashby?"

Now why did that sound so wanton?

She turned around again. "I doubt that, my lord. I wanted to play a game of billiards with Papa."

"I might not be as savvy as your Papa, but I dare say I'd make a fair opponent."

He had a sensual glow in his eyes.

She pinched her brows, fearing his proposal some sort of trick. Besides, she didn't want to spend more time with the viscount.

Wait! Perhaps a game of billiards was the ideal opportunity to get the viscount to stay away from her? She was a skilled billiardist. If she made another wager with the viscount—and won, this time—she could wrest from him another promise for a home of her own. Separate apartments would be grand, the best solution to this dreadful predicament.

After a thoughtful pause, she gave a brisk nod. "Very well, Ravenswood."

A few minutes later, Henrietta was hunched over the billiard table, eyeing the ivory cue ball. "Shall we make the game more interesting?"

Sebastian quirked a black brow. "What did you have in mind?"

"Winner gets to make another wish."

He observed her for a moment, his eyes smoky. "All right, Miss Ashby."

Henrietta dismissed the shiver tickling her spine and returned her attention to the cue ball. With a loud crack, the white ball struck the red ball. One point for her.

She moved around to the other side of the table and positioned herself, struck the red ball and nicked Sebastian's cue ball. Two points for her.

She was very good at three-ball. In a short while, she'd have that fashionable apartment in Town.

"Magnificent," he breathed.

Henrietta felt a measure of satisfaction in his words. She was good, true. But magnificent?

"A rump to satisfy a man's hunger."

Henrietta balked. Heat invaded her belly, stormed her breast. She missed the red ball and the cushion, forfeiting a point.

She stood up and glared at Ravenswood. "How dare you?"

But Sebastian wasn't staring at her. He was looking out the window. Apparently, hers was not the rump being admired.

Henrietta followed his gaze to the workers outside, bringing in a boar. Tonight's dinner, no doubt.

She quickly swallowed her outburst.

Sebastian glanced back at the table. "Is it my turn?"

Oh, the knave! He'd done that on purpose, she was sure. To unnerve her, the bounder.

Sebastian arched his splendid form. As he stretched forward, Henrietta couldn't help but admire the hard muscles in his calves or the brawn surging through his arms as he positioned the cue. The lock of hair that dropped over his eye just then only made the man more irresistible.

Blast it!

Sebastian struck the red ball, knocked her cue ball, and scored two points.

Henrietta twisted her lips.

The viscount moved around the table for another shot. "How did you sleep last night, Miss Ashby?"

"Terrible." *Thanks to you,* she thought.

He scored another point. "I figured as much."

"And how did you figure that?" she demanded

Another loud crack as the red ball rolled across the table. "I was out for a walk late last night. I saw the candle burning in your window."

Henrietta took in a sharp breath. He was watching her through her bedroom window! Did he see her undress?

"I was a perfect gentleman, I assure you, Miss Ashby."

She wanted to snort. She composed her features, instead. The man could read her thoughts. What was happening to her? How could he unravel her guard with a little banter? After months of training with Madam Jacqueline, it was very disquieting.

"Why were you so restless, Miss Ashby?"

"I could ask the same of you?"

He moved to the other end of the table, his dark blue eyes on her. "I had a very distressing problem to solve."

"About what?"

"Shopping."

He was funning with her. No man thought about shopping, especially a rake like Ravenswood. He only thought about vice.

"And you, Miss Ashby?" He scored another point. "What kept you awake?"

The relentless attention of an attractive rogue, she mused, still piqued. But she wouldn't tell him that. Instead, she decided to have a bit of fun herself.

"A rat," she said.

"How dreadful."

"It was a stubborn little bugger … but I dashed it to bits."

Sebastian missed his shot.

Henrietta lifted her brows. "Oh, is it my turn?"

She swished her hips and moved to the other end of the table.

She could feel Sebastian's hot gaze on her back the entire time. It seared her right through her clothes.

Henrietta struck the red ball. She missed Sebastian's cue ball, but still, one more point for her.

"A rat, eh?" he said. "I'm surprised you didn't scream."

She snorted. "I would never make such ungodly racket."

"I've heard you make ungodly racket before, Miss Ashby."

She stiffened. The dark timbre of his voice sent shivers down her spine. He was alluding to the night she'd spent in his arms; the cries and groans of sweet passion that he'd ripped from her throat.

She missed her shot.

He said in a soft voice, "I see it's my turn again."

Henrietta meshed her lips together. How could the rogue still affect her so? How could the sound of his watery voice still make her ache for him?

Sebastian made his shot. Two points for him.

She pinched her lips even more. He was trying to make her lose, the blackguard. She had to get a hold of her wits. She had to win this wager if she wanted the bounder to stay away from her.

"Yes, my lord, you are very familiar with ungodly ways, aren't you?"

Sebastian made his shot. He nicked her cue ball. Another two points for him. But he did not return to the game right away. Instead, he propped the end of his cue stick against the ground and rested his hands over the tip.

Henrietta could feel the caress of his eyes. She tried to still the rampant beats of her heart, but his stare only made her even more apprehensive.

"You and I are about to married, Miss Ashby. Perhaps I intend to reform my ungodly ways and start anew?"

"A rogue cannot reform his ways," she countered, her breath uneven. "You're a scoundrel, Ravenswood."

"I was, true, but I think it's time for a change."

"And why change now?"

Sebastian made another shot. One more point for him. Lud!

"We're about to wed, Miss Ashby. A change seems fitting. A fresh start for both of us."

She didn't believe him, but wondered anyway, "And how do you intend to change?"

"Ah, that is the difficult part, so I will need your help, I'm afraid."

Henrietta widened her eyes. "Why do you need my help?"

"Well, I cannot go it alone, Miss Ashby. I need someone to be my moral guide."

"If you want to change your wicked habits, you can do so by yourself."

He lifted a brow. "You mean the way you seduced me without any instruction?"

Her breath hitched. "I never ..."

His head cocked. "You tried."

"That was different."

"How so?"

"It was a foolish mistake. I should never have gone to see Madam Jacqueline."

"You're right, you shouldn't have met the courtesan. It was a terrible blunder, very imprudent."

Was he berating *her* about impropriety? The hypocritical knave! "How dare you!"

"Is something the matter, Miss Ashby? I was only agreeing with you."

She squeezed the cue stick hard. "And what will you do once you've reformed your ways?"

Sebastian took another shot. "Oh, I don't know. Take on the role of straightlaced husband. Have a brat or two. Oh, never mind about the brats. I'm not to touch you—ever. But I'd like to give the ordinary, respectable life a try."

She had the urge to slam her cue stick over the billiard table. The miserable wretch! He was spouting everything she'd wanted to hear from him in the past. But it was all a lie. He was a devious sort. For some nefarious reason, he wanted her to believe him.

Well, she'd do no such thing. She refused to believe a man like Ravenswood could change. It was impossible. He was too much of a scoundrel to ever reform. And even if he changed, the transformation would be short-lived. In a few weeks or months he'd tire of the "ordinary, respectable" life. He'd go back to his vile club and surrender to his degenerate ways. And she was not going to be the wife left behind in tears.

Never!

"Well, Miss Ashby, it looks like I've won."

The bounder was right. He'd scored the most points.

Why did she keep losing every wager?

Sebastian set his cue stick across the billiard's table. "And for your challenge loss, I request your presence … in my bedchamber."

CHAPTER 23

Henrietta stared at Sebastian's closed bedroom door. He had retired from the billiard room ahead of her. What devious scheme had he orchestrated behind the door?

She snorted. A reformed rogue, indeed. He was a villain. He would always be a villain. And whatever ploy he'd fashioned, she'd no intention of submitting to it. She was going to honor her challenge loss by coming to his room. But that was all she was going to do.

Henrietta rapped on the door.

"Enter."

She pushed on the latch and entered the chamber.

"How good of you to join me, Miss Ashby. I was beginning to wonder if you'd come to my room."

He stood beside the bedpost with a shoulder propped against the wood in a very suggestive pose. Worse, he wasn't wearing his coat. His crisp white shirt was stretched across the taut muscles of his strapping chest. And he didn't have a cravat. She spied a tuft of exposed dark curls.

Henrietta was in deep trouble.

"Are you suggesting I would dishonor my word?" she said in an uneven voice.

"I beg your forgiveness, Miss Ashby. I have the utmost faith in you. You would never break your vow."

Sebastian sauntered toward her, each step deliberate and provocative.

"Why have you summoned me here, Ravenswood?"

He pressed his thumb to the swell of her cheek. "I have something for you."

She released a soft gasp at his tender touch. "You do?"

"Something I think you'll like very much."

He was going to kiss her. She could sense it. Her nerves were humming. Well, he was going to get a smack for his impudence. Maybe another bite on the lips, the bounder.

"Close your eyes," he whispered.

Henrietta's lashes fluttered closed. Her lips suddenly pouted ... and something nestled in her hands.

"Open your eyes, Miss Ashby."

She blinked. A black velvet purse rested between her palms.

No kisses?

She twisted her lips. "What is this?"

"A Christmas present."

"Christmas was last week."

"And I apologize for my belated gift."

She wrinkled her brow. "But why are you giving me a present?"

"Can't a man give his betrothed a gift?"

She made a moue.

"Go on," he said. "Open it."

Henrietta slowly opened the purse and reached inside the blackness. Her fingers struck something cold. Glass?

She removed a small glass globe, perched on a wood stand. Inside the globe was two figurines ... dancing. She shook the globe and the water inside swished; little bits of white resin swirled like snow.

It reminded her of the engagement party when she'd danced with Sebastian under the falling snow.

Her heart pinched.

"Do you like it?" he said, eyes intent upon her.

"It's beautiful," she whispered, tears filling her eyes. And if anyone but Sebastian had given her the present, she would have been delighted by the thoughtful gift.

But knowing it came from him—the one who'd crushed all her dreams—made it bittersweet.

Why was he doing this to her? she wondered. He wasn't acting like a rogue. He was acting like the hero she had always wanted him to be. But she knew it was a ruse. And she didn't understand why he was being so cruel.

A cacophony of female voices: her sisters. Shouts about "flowers" and "water" echoed throughout the house. The blooms from the hothouse must have arrived.

"You should go, Miss Ashby, before your sisters discover us together. We don't want to cause another scandal, do we?"

~ * ~

It was growing dark. Sebastian searched the property, looking for Henrietta. She had disappeared from the house a short while ago. He wasn't alarmed, though; he suspected her whereabouts. But he was confused.

Earlier that day, he'd made her tear up with his gift. That was a good thing, right? She must have liked the present … then why was he still avoiding him?

He made a grimace. Henrietta was so *un*like an ordinary lass. It had always been easy for him to see a woman's thoughts in her eyes—but not with Henrietta. He sensed, at times, she wanted his kisses. He also sensed, at other times, she wanted to jab her cue stick into his eye.

The girl was still angry with him. The gift had failed to impress her. What was he going to do now?

Sebastian heard metal blades cutting ice. He spotted the pond … and a lone shadow skating over the icy surface.

He stood back for a minute, watching Henrietta, thinking about the time he had skated in *her* arms. She was so determined to be different. So stubborn, too. And she was spirited. Bedding her would be bliss. If only he could convince her life under the covers with him wouldn't be so abysmal.

Sebastian sauntered to the pond's edge. "It's late."

Henrietta skated to a stop. In the twilight, it was hard to see her eyes, but he could *feel* her fierce stare.

"What are you doing here, Ravenswood?"

"I've come to escort you back to the house," he said. "It's almost dinner."

"I'm not hungry."

She skated off, the willful chit.

Sebastian glared after her. He couldn't follow her onto the ice; he had no skates. He had to find some other way to coax her off the frozen pond.

"Miss Ashby, I cannot leave you alone on the ice."

He had to raise his voice since she'd skated to the pond's *other* edge.

"And why not?" came the indignant retort.

"Because I am a gentleman, Miss Ashby, and I cannot abandon you in the wilderness."

She had beguiled him once with just such a rejoinder. Now he had used her own words against her. Apparently, she didn't appreciate that, for he heard her snort across the pond.

He said, "Your father would have my head if I let you get eaten by a wild animal."

Was that a "good riddance" he'd heard?

Sebastian sighed. She was going to be *very* obstinate, wasn't she?

"It's getting dark," he tried next. "You won't be able to find your way back home."

"I can *see* the lights from the house."

True. Blast it! It appeared he didn't have any other choice but to go after the mulish girl.

Sebastian tested the ice with the tip of his boot. He didn't fare too well with skating blades. Perhaps he might fare better without them?

He would soon find out.

With a tentative step, he set one boot on the ice.

Still standing.

He took another step.

Again, he was still standing.

Encouraged, he slid one boot in front of the other.

Big mistake.

Sebastian landed on his rump with a wicked thump.

A bit dazed, it took him a moment to hear the lyrical laughter.

So the vixen took pleasure in his foolery? Strange, but he didn't mind her laughter. It was musical and rather infectious, and he found himself grinning, too. Good thing it was too dark for her to see. He didn't want her to think he enjoyed making an ass of himself.

But so long as she wasn't crying or cursing him, he was content to let her have her fun.

"I'm glad you're amused, Miss Ashby."

"Encore!" she giggled.

Sebastian staggered and tried to regain his balance. "Didn't you once promise to catch me if I fall?"

"And you believed me?"

The impudence.

"It looks like I need your help, Miss Ashby."

"Rot!"

"I need you for balance, I'm afraid."

She humphed.

"Really, Miss Ashby, I'm stranded without you."

She was quiet for a moment, then said, "Just crawl back to shore."

"A man of my station on his hands and knees? Outrageous."

She skated to the center of the ice, but no further. "You would rather a mere chit assist you?"

"I would rather my betrothed assist me."

She was silent again.

"You have a way of getting into trouble, Ravenswood," she said after a brief pause.

As do you, he reflected, but thought it prudent to keep the sentiment to himself.

"Does this mean you'll help me, Miss Ashby?"

She huffed. "I suppose so."

A loud crack.

Sebastian scrambled to his knees. "Henry, don't move!"

Henrietta froze.

But it happened again; the ice splinter.

"Sebastian!"

"Henry, be still!" he cried. "I'm coming!"

Sebastian crawled across the ice. The vilest hurt hacked at his breast, taking his breath away.

"I'm almost there, Henry."

Another fracture.

She let out a sob. "Sebastian, hurry!"

The fright in her voice twisted his innards. He scrambled across the ice as fast as he could. But he didn't want to put too much pressure on the thinning sheet. It might shatter before he reached Henrietta.

It was too late, though.

Another loud snap.

Henrietta looked up at him, her eyes glossy wet with tears, before the ice gave way, and she plummeted into the dark depths with a shrill scream.

"Henry!"

Sebastian, wild with fear, dropped to his belly and carefully slid across the frozen pond.

Henrietta thrashed in the frigid waters, but her winter clothes were like an anchor, dragging her underwater.

The shrieks stopped.

She slipped below the waterline.

"Henry!"

Sebastian reached the hole in the ice and plunged his arm into the freezing pond. He searched for her, frantic. And then he felt it. Soggy wool. He grabbed her by the scruff of her cape, hoisting her to the surface

Henrietta gasped for air. It was the sweetest sound he had ever heard.

"Oh God, Henry!"

Sebastian yanked her through the hole in the ice. Her teeth chatted and cracked like fireworks. She was so cold to the touch. Her skin was pale. Her lips were blue. He had to get her into the house. Fast.

He cradled her in his arms. "Hang on, Henry."

It was too risky to stand. The ice might split even more. He had to drag her across the fragile surface, keep the weight on the ice even.

Sebastian reached the pond's edge at last. He shrugged the greatcoat off his shoulders, and wrapped it around Henrietta. She was shaking so hard; her sweet eyes shut tight.

He scooped her in his arms. "Don't you dare leave me, Henry."

He kissed her chilled brow and started to run toward the house.

CHAPTER 24

Henrietta was feeling much better. She sat on a divan, wrapped in a blanket, observing the winter landscape from the parlor window.

It had been two days since the accident on the ice. She needed respite from her fussing family, and the solitude in the parlor offered her a chance to reflect.

Sebastian had saved her life. He had pulled her from the frigid water. And she was grateful to him. Truly, she was. But a part of her still mistrusted him.

The viscount was heralded a hero. The whole household was in accord. Even her sisters believed him more of a saint than a sinner. And while Henrietta didn't disapprove of the accolades, she was confused. Had the man really changed? Could such a renowned scoundrel reform his wicked ways?

The parlor door opened.

"You have a visitor, Miss Ashby."

Henrietta eyed the butler. "Who is it, Wilkes?"

"Lord Emerson."

Ah, yes, the young gentleman from the engagement bash. "Show him in, Wilkes."

A short while later Emerson was holding a cup of tea and smiling. "You look well, Miss Ashby. I can't tell you how relieved I am to see you recovered."

"Thank you, my lord." She smiled in return. "I appreciate the well wishes."

"It's been the talk of the countryside, you know? Your little mishap."

Little?

"You must promise never to go out on the ice again," he said.

"I think that's rather much, my lord."

"Really, Miss Ashby. If I were your betrothed, I would forbid you from ice skating."

Henrietta frowned. "My lord—"

"You are too precious to lose, Miss Ashby."

She sighed. He was not the most debonair of men, so curt and authoritative. But she supposed his intention to protect her was honorable, albeit misplaced. "Thank you, my lord."

"How is your father, my lord?"

"The earl?" Emerson sipped his tea. "Bedridden, I'm afraid."

"I'm sorry to hear that."

"Don't be, Miss Ashby. The earl is strong willed. He's too stubborn to die."

Too stubborn to die? How strange! But she soon dismissed his discourteous answer when she heard:

"I must say, Miss Ashby, I'm impressed by your talent."

"My talent?"

"You've tamed London's most renowned bachelor."

Henrietta wasn't so sure about that. Ravenswood tamed? Not with a whip and a ring of fire … but then again, the viscount *was* acting like a gentleman.

Oh, Henrietta didn't know what to think anymore!

"Ravenswood riveted?" he said. "I'm astonished, really. I believed him a lifelong bachelor. But, if I might be so bold, you are very tempting bait, Miss Ashby."

Tempting indeed. She had bungled everything. If she hadn't penned that silly letter to Ravenswood, she wouldn't be in this bind.

Henrietta ignored Emerson's false flattery, curious, instead, about the man's association with her betrothed. "Do you know the viscount well, my lord?"

"Not at all." He flicked his fingers. "I just read the papers."

She pinched her brows. "The papers?"

"The society pages. Rumor has it ... Oh, listen to me prattle about idle gossip. It's most inappropriate. Do forgive me, Miss Ashby."

"Yes, of course, my lord," she murmured.

Society pages? Rumors? A tight knot formed in her belly. A reformed rogue, indeed! What sort of scandal was her scoundrel of a betrothed embroiled in now? And to think she had considered the idea of his transformation!

"I don't know how these rumors ever get started," said Emerson. "But it's good to know the tittle-tattle is all nonsense. You are a miracle worker, Miss Ashby. The whole *ton* agrees."

Oh good, she was a spectacle. A sideshow amusement. She could hear the showman now: come and see the miracle worker tame the beast Ravenswood. It was all rubbish. If she had any sway over the rebellious viscount, the man would *not* be in the society papers!

"Well, Miss Ashby, I've taken up enough of your time." Emerson stood. "I wish you good day."

"Good day, my lord."

He gave a curt bow, then quit the room.

Henrietta twisted her lips. She picked up the porcelain bell on the table beside her and shook it for all she was worth.

The butler appeared. "You rang, Miss Ashby?"

"Wilkes, do we have a copy of the paper?"

"I believe so."

"Will you fetch it for me?"

"Right away, Miss Ashby."

The butler left the room—and Henrietta stewed.

The wily bounder! How could Ravenswood do this to her? Expose her to gossip and ridicule? She had asked him to keep his immoral behavior a secret, to hide his lecherous conduct from polite society. But it seemed he was too much a villain to grant her even that simple wish.

Henrietta took in a shaky breath, her heart fluttering. She was right to mistrust the viscount. She was right to think him a knave. The man was a gentleman in name alone. He hadn't a scrap of respect for her.

The butler soon returned with the broadsheets. "Here you are, Miss Ashby."

"Thank you, Wilkes."

"Will there be anything else?"

"No, that will be all, Wilkes."

The butler bowed and once more left the room.

Henrietta peeled back the pages of the paper, her fingers trembling. She scanned the society section, looking for any mention of Ravenswood.

At length she saw the snippet of gossip:

… and now for a festive bit of news. A confirmed bachelor is prepared to take wedding vows on Twelfth Night. How romantic! One has to applaud the bride for her charm and beauty—and her clever wiles. A friend near and dear to the groom purports the gentleman vowed never to marry, but the lady in question enchanted him until he proposed … although I hear the groom might be disenchanted after the wedding. Oh, the trials of matrimony!

Henrietta saw red. The scheming bounder! How could he besmirch her like that? Imply she'd "enchanted" him into bed to get a proposal, and then intended to neglect his husbandly needs? Did he think to humiliate her into wifely submission?

A near and dear friend, indeed. It was the viscount who had spread the vile tale. She had told no one but him of her intention to marry in name alone, so he had to have spread the rumor himself.

Henrietta slapped the paper against the tabletop. "Curse him!"

"Curse who, Miss Ashby?"

Ravenswood was at the door, looking dapper as ever. And she wanted to scratch out his eyes.

"No one of consequence," she gritted.

He swaggered into the parlor, unperturbed by her display of pique, and settled into a chair. "You look well, Miss Ashby."

Well, she felt like a dunce. Ravenswood was a scoundrel. He would never change. He would charm and flirt and spin yarns of treachery to get what he wanted, but he would never be true or good or trustworthy.

"I have something for you, Miss Ashby."

He slipped out of the chair and kneeled.

"What are you doing?" she said, alarmed.

"It occurred to me we haven't had a proper courtship." He rummaged in his pocket and removed a ring. "And since we are starting anew, Miss Ashby, I think this might be appropriate."

Henrietta blinked. The shimmering emerald was a square cut, set in yellow gold. It was stunning … breathtaking … "Beautiful."

He slipped the ring over her finger. "I'm glad you think so. It belonged to my mother, and I'd like you to have it. Think of it as an engagement ring."

Henrietta eyed the dazzling bauble … and quickly realized the viscount was up to his old ways: charming and flirting and spinning yarns.

She slipped the ring off her finger. "I can't accept this."

"And why not?"

"Because we're not going to have a real marriage. Our union will be in name alone."

The flinch in his cheek indicated he was upset by the news. But Henrietta wasn't going to let him think he'd earned a place in her bed just because he'd saved her life. Gratitude was one thing, enslaving her heart was another.

"You should keep the ring, Ravenswood."

"And give it to whom? You are going to be my wife, Miss Ashby. You are the only wife I will ever have."

Henrietta gathered her valor and returned the jewelry. "I'm sorry, but I can't take the ring."

"I see." He pressed his lips together.

She wanted to sink under the blanket, his stare was so smoldering. Instead, she gathered the coverlet close to her breast.

He pocketed the ring. "I'm sorry, too, Miss Ashby. I thought the ring would be appreciated. Forgive my impudence."

He looked more furious than repentant, though, and Henrietta loathed to hurt him. He had saved her life, after all. And she'd give him the gratitude he deserved. That much she would do.

"Since you are here, Ravenswood, I must thank you."

He lifted off his haunches and growled, "For what?"

"For saving my life, of course."

"Oh? So you've noticed?"

"What rubbish! Of course, I've noticed."

"Well, you're welcome. I hope you're feeling better, Miss Ashby?"

"I am," she said, trying to sound calm, but feeling dreadfully guilty on the inside for being so uncouth. "Thank you for asking, my lord."

Yet why was she feeling guilty? She had every right to keep Ravenswood at bay. His charm only increased with each passing day. And Henrietta had to guard her heart. He was an irredeemable rogue. The vicious gossip he had spread in the paper was proof of that.

"Good day, Ravenswood."

"Good day, Miss Ashby."

Quietly he walked out of the room.

CHAPTER 25

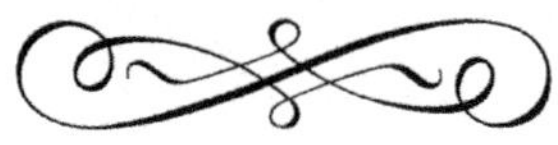

Sebastian sat in the library, the broadsheets spread across his lap. It was late. There was only a fire in the room, crackling, spitting, hissing. He watched the blaze, transfixed.

He had suspected something was amiss earlier in the day, when he'd first walked into the parlor and observed Henrietta cursing and smacking the furniture with the newspaper. Her subsequent cold manner had told him something was *definitely* amiss, and as soon as he'd recovered the paper, he'd realized what that something was. No wonder she was furious with him. The gossip might not mention him or her my name, but the "wedding vows on Twelfth Night" gave away their identities. And knowing Henrietta's wary nature, she probably assumed *he* had voiced the vicious sentiments.

"There you are, Seb." His brother sauntered into the room and headed straight for the liquor cabinet. "Brandy?"

"No."

"No brandy?" He set the decanter aside. "Are you feeling all right?"

Sebastian tossed the paper across the room. "Read that, Peter."

Peter placed his drink on the table, picked up the newsprint, and held it close to the firelight. "Read what?"

"The snippet near the bottom."

After a silent moment, Peter whistled. "Tough luck, old boy." He took the tumbler and sat down next to his brother on the settee. "How did that get into the paper?"

"Deuce if I know."

"Is the story true?" asked Peter.

"That Henrietta doesn't want me to share the marriage bed? I'm afraid so."

"Now that's *really* tough luck, old boy." Peter shook his head in commiseration. "By and by, who is this 'near and dear' friend?"

"Probably the same scoundrel who bandied Henrietta's letter all over Town. Someone's been eavesdropping on my private conversations with the chit."

"Ah, you have an enemy … but then again you must have so many enemies."

Sebastian glared at his brother. "Are you trying to be helpful, Peter? If you are, sod off!"

Peter chuckled. "All right, I'll be helpful. How shall we discover the identity of this scoundrel?"

"Forget about the scoundrel. I'll deal with him later, whoever he is. First I have to mollify my betrothed."

"Why don't you offer her a present?"

"I tried that, Peter. I gave her Mother's emerald ring. A fat lot of good it did me, though. She threw the bauble back in my face."

Peter sighed. "I wish I could be more obliging, Seb, but I don't know the working of a woman's heart. I misjudge my own wife more'n half the time." He took a swig of brandy. "You know who we need right now?"

"Who?"

"Father."

Sebastian creased his brow. "Why Father?"

"Because Father was a philosopher," said Peter. "Don't you remember? He always had a ready quip from a psalm or poem or some other sage canon."

Sebastian remembered all right. He remembered being a boy, interred within the schoolroom on a glorious summer day, reciting from the texts of historians and philosophers and scientists.

A disciplinarian, Father had served as both parent and teacher, determined to fill the young minds of his sons with clever doctrines. He'd espoused truths and mores with frightening fervor. And he'd expected his offspring to obey the teachings, to live by them. Not a violent man, their father was nonetheless capable of instilling fear. And to two impressionable boys, the imposing image of the former viscount had made a lasting impression. To this day, Sebastian could still flinch at the memory of his father's glower.

"I bet Father would have a verse to debunk the mystery of a woman's heart," said Peter.

"Well, if Father had such a poetic verse, it didn't do him much good."

"What do you mean?"

"He and Mother didn't have the best rapport, Peter."

"Rubbish! Mother was very happy."

"Mother was rich."

Peter pinched his brows. "So?"

"So she spent her days shopping—far away from Father."

"Father wasn't that disagreeable, Seb."

"Oh, no? Don't you remember our time in the schoolroom, dissecting the *History of Rome,* while every other young scamp was out and about, looking up ladies' skirts?"

Peter scoffed. "You make childhood sound so miserable. Father used to take us on outings in the country, don't you remember?"

"To instruct us on flora and fauna."

"What about the trip to Rome? It was an aimable sojourn."

"We spent the entire time in a monastery learning Latin. It was hardly an aimable sojourn."

Peter made a moue. "You have a selective memory, Seb."

"You have a defective one, brother."

"Do you really think so?" Peter frowned. "Do you think I've buried the unpleasant memories?"

"I do," said Sebastian. "Now if only I could do the same."

Peter glanced at him askance. "What do you mean?"

Sebastian shut his eyes for a moment, then: "Do you remember what Father used to say about good and evil?"

"No."

"He used to say that some of us were born good and destined to return to heaven, while others were born damned. That there was nothing one could do about his fate. If you were born damned, all the good deeds in creation couldn't save you."

Peter nodded. "Ah, yes, the idea of predestination. I remember now."

"Do you think Father was right?"

Peter shrugged. "It's church dogma, centuries old."

"Does being old make the theory untrue?"

"Well, no, but it doesn't make it true, either."

"I was just wondering."

Peter glanced at his brother again. "Did you take that theory to heart?"

Sebastian looked at the hearth and inhaled the scent of burning wood. He wanted to deny it, but, in truth, he *had* taken the theory to heart. Considering his wicked disposition, he'd reasoned he was one of the damned, and redemption was impossible, good works fruitless. Long ago, he'd resigned himself to his fate.

But now… now he didn't want to be doomed anymore. His parents had suffered a lonely sham of a marriage. He didn't want the same cursed destiny. But how to get Henrietta to trust him?

Change his dastardly ways?

Sebastian snorted.

Could a scoundrel really reform his ways? After everything he had done for Henrietta, she still loathed him, considered him a fiend. Perhaps he was one? Perhaps that's why she didn't want anything to do with him anymore? Perhaps she could see him for what he really was and always would be—a villain? And mayhap all the good deeds in creation couldn't change that truth?

"Listen, Seb." Peter elbowed his brother in the ribs. "I know Father was an important figure in our lives, but don't let what he said so many years ago shape your life today."

Sebastian mulled that over. Even if his brother was right, it did not negate the fact that he was still a rogue. It was what he was good at …

Well, then, perhaps it was time Sebastian put the rogue inside him to good use? He had saved Henrietta's life, offered her gifts, acted the gentleman, and she still rebuffed him. Good deeds did not impress her. Perhaps she wanted something a little more … scandalous?

Did she still desire his kisses? If so, Sebastian was going to give them to her.

CHAPTER 26

Henrietta set down the candle. Feeling a pinch of remorse, she opened the black velvet purse and removed the glass globe, carefully placing it on the mantelpiece.

Sebastian was not going to like finding it there when he returned to his room. He was going to be furious, she was sure.

But Henrietta had to return the present. She should never have accepted it in the first place. She didn't care for the viscount. To keep such a gift suggested their engagement was meaningful, that their marriage would be, too. But that was not the case. And she didn't wanted Sebastian to think otherwise.

She picked up the candle, about to tiptoe from the room, when she shrieked and dropped the light

Sebastian stomped on the candle, dousing the flame.

"Good evening, Miss Ashby."

Oh, that husky male voice! It made her shiver right down to her toes.

"Forgive the intrusion, Ravenswood. I was just ..."

Sebastian took the poker beside the hearth and stabbed at the dwindling flames, stoking the fire.

"You were just what?" he asked.

The dark room brightened—and the glass globe glowed.

Henrietta chewed on her bottom lip, dreading the inevitable quarrel, but Sebastian didn't notice the globe. Oh, no. He noticed her, instead.

"Have you come to bed, Miss Ashby?"

She gasped. "No, I have not!"

"Pity," was all that he said.

"How dare you assume—"

"Miss Ashby," he said in a dark timbre, lips so low she could feel his warm breath on her cheeks. "When I find a beautiful woman in my room, so scantily attired, I must assume she has come to bed."

A confused Henrietta peeked at her ensemble and stifled another gasp. She was dressed in her night rail and wrapper! It'd wholly slipped her mind.

Quickly she gripped the wrapper by the collar, hiding her breasts.

He tsked. "It's not like you, Miss Ashby, to be so bashful."

"And it's just like you to be such a scoundrel."

He grinned. The audacious man actually grinned.

"What happened to the gentleman inside you?"

"He went away."

"Oh, did he now?"

"You chased him away, I'm afraid."

"And how did I do that?"

"By coming to my room so late at night."

She trembled at his whispered words; gooseflesh spread across her body. "If you will excuse me, my lord."

"Do you really want to go?"

He traced the line of her brow with his thumb, rounded her eye, then stroked the top of her cheek in a sensual caress.

"I think you'd rather stay," he murmured.

Her uneven breath quickened when he bussed her brow. She was rooted to the spot. She had wanted this—*him*—for such a long time. And while her heart said "run," her body screamed "stay." Stay and touch him. Stay and take him!

"I think you want to be with me, Henry."

Her lashes fluttered closed as he bussed the ridge of her nose. Her nickname had never sounded so right!

"I think you want me to make love to you," he said in *the* most seducing voice. And then he brushed her lips with his warm mouth.

It shouldn't feel so good to be kissed by him, she thought. He was a scoundrel. He had devastated her heart.

But it did feel good.

So achingly good.

"Do you, Henry? Do you want me to make love to you?"

She arched on her toes; a hair's breadth from his sinful lips. But she wouldn't admit her desire for him. It would only give him clout over her. She wanted his kisses, though. So much it pained her breast.

"Sebastian," she breathed instead.

His mouth came down hard over hers.

Oh, mercy! The heat. The pleasure. She wanted to drop her wrapper right there on the ground, and take him into her arms.

"I know you, Henry," he breathed between kisses, suckling her bottom lip. Nipping at it, too. "I know what you like." The moist tip of his tongue skimmed her swollen lips. "You like to watch, don't you? You like to look at pictures in books."

He broke away from the sensuous kiss.

Henrietta was about to have a snit in protest.

But Sebastian slowly pushed her back against the bedpost—and unfastened his trousers. "Look at me, Henry." He took her by the hand. "I want you to see what you do to me."

Henrietta gasped at the hard length of him in her palm. After looking at all those luscious men in Madam Jacqueline's naughty book of pictures, she was dizzy with passion, moist with intense arousal to see Sebastian's nakedness.

He nuzzled her temple and said in a throaty whisper, "Do you see what you do to me?"

He thickened in her hand.

Henrietta bit her bottom lip to keep from groaning.

He nipped her earlobe. "Do you see how you make me feel?"

She shuddered in his embrace, undone.

"Take off my robe," she demanded.

"With pleasure, my little despot."

And he pulled the garment off her shoulders, letting it fall to the floor.

"What do I make you feel?" He flicked his tongue over her mouth. "Tell me, Henry."

Henrietta didn't want to admit the truth; to open her heart to him. She just wanted to open her body to him—for one night.

She arched on her toes again, reaching for his lips.

But he did not kiss her.

"Tell me, Henry. Tell me what I make you feel."

He pushed her hand away from his erection. He pressed her up against the bedpost instead … and started to rock his hips.

Oh, sweet heaven!

"I'll make the ache inside you go away, Henry. Tell me what you feel."

Her resolve cracked under the pressure of her need to be with Sebastian, and she cried out, "Hungry."

He kissed her. "What else do I make you feel?"

She gasped. "Wet."

He thrust against her again. "What else?"

"Frightened," she said weakly.

Sebastian took her lips in his for a thorough kiss. "I promise, Henry, you won't be frightened of me after tonight—ever again."

She wanted to believe him. Her heart ached for those words to be true.

He scooped her in his arms and set her down on the bed. He rucked her night rail up to her waist and nestled between her thighs.

Henrietta moaned as the cusp of his erection nudged the moist folds of her tender flesh.

He said in a ragged whisper, "Do you like this, Henry?"

"Truthfully … I don't."

Sebastian stiffened. Slowly he eased out of her.

"But I thought …" He looked dumbfounded. "Henry, I thought you wanted me to—"

"No," she said, then nipped at his bottom lip. She held his lip in her mouth for a moment before she slowly let it slip between her teeth. "I'd much rather be on top."

His nostrils flared. With a violent shudder, Sebastian yanked her to her feet, and dragged her over to the cushy armchair by the crackling fire. He kicked the ottoman away and settled in the seat.

"Come here," he bade.

She splayed her legs and straddled him.

"Is this better?" he growled.

She couldn't resist a smug grin. "Much."

He humphed, not amused by the little trick she'd played a moment ago. But he deserved as much, the rogue, for teasing her senses in such a cruel fashion. And now that she had the advantage of being on top of him, she was rife with adoration and curiosity.

"Take off your shirt," she bade him this time.

He pulled the garment over his head and tossed it away. Her hands trembled as she stroked the man's corded muscles, the dark curls on his chest, rough to the touch. She raked her fingers through those curls and stroked the hard nubs of his nipples.

"You're so beautiful," she whispered, awed.

She bussed his brow and inhaled the intoxicating fragrance of Eau de Cologne.

He grabbed her rump and pressed her harder against his erection—but she resisted taking him inside her. She pushed his shoulders and looked right into his fiery eyes.

"How do I make you feel?" she whispered.

He tensed.

She nipped his bottom lip.

He growled.

She nipped him again. "Tell me."

"Hungry," he gritted.

She bussed him again. "What else?"

"Hard."

She dropped her brow and nuzzled him. "What else?"

He whispered, "Frightened."

She opened herself to him then. She pulled her night rail over her head, giving him her breasts, her hips, her ever patch of skin.

"Kiss me," she beseeched.

He kissed her.

"Touch me," she demanded.

His palm circled a swollen breast, thumbed her sensitive nipple, and then, oh sweet mercy, he took her breast into his mouth and sucked the tender flesh.

She dropped her head back, her locks cascading over her spine, and groaned. "Oh, Sebastian!"

She twisted her fingers into his hair, holding him to her breast, while his strong hands rubbed her backside.

Henrietta undulated against him, simulating the same tortuous thrusts he'd tormented her with minutes ago.

"You vixen," he growled, and cupped her hips, guiding her down his pulsing erection.

Henrietta stiffened.

"Don't, Henry," he breathed. "It'll hurt more if you're tight."

Well, *that* didn't make her feel better.

He slipped his fingers between her legs. "It's all right, Henry."

Henrietta bucked.

Sebastian chuckled. "Did you like that?"

Did she like it? More than he would ever know. She had dreamed about being with him for so long. She had ached for him. And she was sure she would never feel such pleasure with any other man.

He thrust inside her. She released a deep breath and eased her muscles over him, taking him deeper and deeper into her womb—and then she rocked over him.

Sebastian guided her every thrust, moaning, and as her need swelled, he too rocked her in quick, piercing strokes. He was breathing hard. The sweat on his brow glistened under the glow of firelight.

It was rapturous, being one with Sebastian, and when the pressure between her legs reached a breaking point, she opened her mouth to cry out in ecstasy.

Sebastian silenced her with a firm kiss, though.

She groaned against his lips, sinking her fingernails into his arms as a burst of energy washed over her, sating her. What glorious relief!

He pumped into her, so deep, before he shuddered, pouring himself into her with a feral groan.

It was over. For a few minutes, Henrietta couldn't move. She held Sebastian, gasping for air, trying to ease the thundering beats of her heart.

"Henry," he whispered, stroking the damp ridges of her spine. "It'll be like this forever."

Henrietta took in a hard breath. Forever? With Sebastian? No. There was no such thing as forever. Not with a man like Sebastian.

Good heavens, what had she done?

~ * ~

Henrietta pushed away from him.

"Where are you going, Henry?"

"I'm going back to my room," she whispered. "I have to be in my own bed come morning."

"Stay," he whispered and pulled her warm body back into his arms. "A little longer."

He bussed her throat, feeling her quickened pulse. She tasted so damn good. And he lapped the briny sweat from her throat … the soft arch of her shoulders.

Was his little despot moaning for more?

The sound of her arousal stoked his wolfish pride. She needed him … like he needed her.

He shuddered at the thought. She was going to be his wife—funny how that word didn't seem so ghastly anymore. And he was going to spend the rest of his days bedding her … holding her … kissing her.

He took her lips in his mouth, his blood burning with the desire to ravish her once more. He stroked her rump, the small of her backside. He kissed her over and over again with passion—and then she pushed at him again.

"What is it, Henry?" he asked in a ragged voice.

"This is a mistake."

"What?"

She tensed. "Us."

His muscles hardened. "What do you mean?"

She scrambled off his lap and reached for her wrapper, covering her beautiful body. "It was a mistake being with you tonight."

A mistake? He had given the woman his body, even his heart, and she called it a "mistake"?

He fastened his trousers and shot out of the chair. "I don't believe you," he growled.

"It's true," she said. "I'm sorry, Sebastian. I never should have come here."

She headed for the door.

He blocked her path.

"You're lying, Henry."

"No, I'm not."

But the flux in her voice told him otherwise. The stubborn chit. Did she mean to torment him? Bed him and then leave him? Did she think to deny him such exquisite pleasure all the rest of her days? Deny herself the same delight? She had enjoyed their mating as much as he had. How was *she* going to live without his touch?

He captured her in a protective hold. Her wrapper fell open, revealing part of her breast. She was so bewitching with her tousled hair and rosy lips. He wanted her again so much it hurt.

"Tell me again this is a mistake." He raked her swollen lips, rounded her hip with his palm. "Tell me you don't want my touch." He slipped his hand inside her robe, caressed her waist … and kneaded her plump breast.

She groaned.

"You want me, Henry," he said roughly between kisses. "I know you do."

"I can't do this, Sebastian," she whimpered. "It's wrong!"

She staggered, then stared at him with a rapacious look in her eyes before she cinched her wrapper and skirted from the room.

Sebastian stood in the middle of the chamber, desperate for breath. Why had she come to his room if she hadn't wanted sex? How could she run from him after the night they'd shared? And then he saw it: the glimmer of glass.

He walked over to the mantle and picked up the glass globe. So that's why she'd come to his room. To return his gift.

Sebastian thumbed the glass, fury rising in his belly, then smashed the globe against the brick hearth. The glass shattered. The water doused the fire. And he was left alone. In the dark.

CHAPTER 27

Henrietta moved across the grounds, enjoying a morning stroll. Her body still burned for Sebastian, and she needed the cool winter air to quench her desire. She had been so sure that a night of coupling would slake the hunger in her belly. But it did nothing of the sort. If anything, she yearned for the viscount even more.

What was she going to do now?

Oh, she was a mess inside! It'd felt so good to be with Sebastian. A part of her had no regrets about the other night. After years of longing, to be with the man was a welcomed relief.

But another part of her was filled with remorse. She'd had a taste of sweet pleasure last night. And she wanted to feel those warm sentiments again and again. Yet she couldn't let a scoundrel like Ravenswood so close to her heart. The man had lied to her, spread a dreadful tale about her in the scandal sheets. He only wanted a tussle in bed. Maybe two or three. But after he'd had his fill of her, he'd abandon her. Retreat to his old haunts. Devastate her.

She had to be more diligent in her rebuff. She could not let her flighty emotions get in the way of reason. She did not care for the man. She lusted after him, true. But the one had nothing to do with the other. Madam Jacqueline had said so herself. It was wholly possible to desire a man and yet dislike him.

But how was she going to forget the sensuous taste of his lips? The incredible thrust of him so deep inside her? How was she going to dismiss his sultry voice from her mind or his spicy touch from her skin?

"Henry!"

Henrietta hardened. "How did you find me?"

Sebastian ambled down the snowy hill. "I followed your footsteps."

Oh, curse her treacherous heart! It cramped at the handsome sight of him. "What are you doing here, Ravenswood?"

He kissed her.

Henrietta gasped in outrage … then moaned with pleasure as the blood in her veins surged and gooseflesh spread all over her body.

Did she have to enjoy the man's kisses so much? Did all her wits have to desert her when he kissed her so?

He let go of her lips—far too soon.

Reason intruded.

Breathless, she demanded, "Why did you kiss me?"

"Every time you call me 'Ravenswood' or 'my lord' or some other infernal title, I'm going to kiss you. I don't care if the whole *ton* is there to witness it. You *will* call me Sebastian."

"You wouldn't dare!"

There was a dark glow in his sea blue eyes. A glow of passion. Of intent. "I most certainly would, Henry."

"Fine," she gritted. "What are you doing here, *Sebastian*?"

"Why did you give back the gift?"

"I can't accept the present. You and I can never truly be husband and wife."

"Why?"

"Because you don't want a wife. You just want a warm body in your bed."

"Is that so?"

"Do you deny it?"

"No, I don't deny it. And why shouldn't I want my wife's warm body in my bed?"

"You've been lying to me this whole time, haven't you?"

"Damn it, Henry!"

"You've only been acting the part of the gentleman to get me to submit to your will. You even spread that ghastly gossip in the paper to try and get your way."

"Now *that* I did not do," he vowed.

"Then who did?"

"I don't know."

"Probably the same scoundrel who flaunted my letter all over Town."

"That's right! Believe me, Henry!"

"I don't believe you. And it was a mistake being with you last tonight. I don't care for you, Sebastian … and I don't want to pretend like I do."

His nostrils flared. "You cared for me last night. You *wanted* me last night."

"I wanted your body, not you."

That struck a sensitive chord. He looked positively livid.

"A woman can lust after a man, too," she said. "*You* should know how easy it is to feel a fire in your belly, but nothing in your heart."

A sharp pang gripped her breast at her own words. Apparently, it wasn't so easy for her to feel a fire in her belly and nothing in her heart.

The man looked haggard. "What do you want from me, Henry?"

"I want you to leave me alone."

He flinched at the word "alone."

"You didn't want me to leave you alone last night. You enjoyed rutting with me, admit it!"

She cringed at his vulgarity. He was angry, lashing out. Still, she didn't like the idea of "rutting" with him. She'd rather think about him …

What? Making love to her? That was almost as nasty a thought, for it implied an emotion. And Henrietta was trying so hard *not* to get emotional.

"I want to forget about last night," she said, tamping the hurt in her breast. "I want to live apart from you once we're wed."

"No."

"Sebastian, I don't want to pretend—"

"We're not going to pretend, damn it! You're going to be *my* wife. You will live under *my* roof. And you will sleep in *my* bed."

She met his steely stare. "Then I suppose you'll have to force me to your bed, for I won't go willing again."

Sebastian took in a hard breath. "You want to live apart from me, do you? What about a child?"

"What child?"

"You might be enceinte, Henry."

That's true. She might have a babe ... but that didn't change anything. "Then I will raise the child alone."

"You would deny me my own child!"

"You're not fit to be a father, Sebastian. What will you do with a son? Teach him to be a 'friar' at your club? What about a daughter? Will you raise her to be part of the demimonde? A 'nun,' perhaps?"

He looked genuinely appalled. "You think me such a fiend?"

"Yes!" Tears welled in her eyes. "I think you're wicked. And if I have a child, I won't let you hurt the babe."

"I don't want to hurt the babe!" He dug his fingers in his hair and let out a curse. "Blast it, is living with me really such a terrible fate?"

The tears burned her cheeks. "Yes!"

"Why?"

"Because I ..."

He took her by the shoulders. "Tell me, Henry. Tell me why?"

"I can't forget."

"Forget what?"

"You … in that abbey … with that woman."

Sebastian sighed. "Henry, listen. It won't be like that anymore. I won't go back to the club, I promise."

"No." she wrested free of his hold. He wanted to get under her skirts, to beguile her into believing he'd honorable intentions. "I won't let you charm me into some sort of trap. I don't trust you, Sebastian. I will never trust you … not with my heart."

Henrietta lifted her skirts to dash through the snow, tears stinging in her eyes. But she didn't care. She had to get away from Sebastian. She had to get away from his promise of redemption.

A promise he couldn't keep.

~ * ~

"The little slut," Emerson grumbled.

He turned his horse around and nudged the beast's flanks, galloping away. He had come to see the wench, to gauge how the piece of *on-dit* he'd planted in the paper had affected her. But it'd had no effect on her at all, it seemed.

The harlot! It was bad enough he'd had to wade through the muck of winter looking for her, but to find her in that bastard's arms! She didn't even care about the foul gossip he'd spread, curse her.

Emerson nudged his horse to ride faster, seething. Yesterday she'd looked ready to skin the viscount alive. But today she was kissing him. It was just like a woman to be so fickle. And it burned in Emerson's gut to know his plan to destroy the couple had failed. Once more, Emerson found himself humiliated at the hands of the viscount. It was more than he could bear.

He would not let Ravenswood win again. He vowed to destroy the viscount; to make the man feel the misery of defeat. And he was going to use that hussy Miss Ashby to do it. If Ravenswood wanted the little strumpet, then

Emerson was going to take her away from him—by any means necessary.

An hour later, Emerson returned to Ormsby Manor. He handed the horse's reins to the stableboy and entered the house, rife with newfound resolve. But his curmudgeon of a father put a swift end to that.

"Is that you, you blundering numskull?"

Emerson hardened. The clip-clop of the earl's cane resounded throughout the hall.

"Yes, Father," he growled.

The old miser hobbled into the foyer, cranky as ever. "Where have you been?"

Emerson gritted, "I was tending to a personal affair."

"What was it? A gaming debt? I'll not give you more money!" The earl brandished his cane. "Mark my words. I'll let you rot in debtors' prison first!"

Emerson sidestepped the earl.

"Come back here, you varlet of a son."

But Emerson ignored the earl and mounted the steps instead, grinding his teeth.

"A pox on you!" the earl cried. "You're nothing but a disgrace. I'll not leave you my estate. I'll live forever! See if I don't."

And he was just spiteful enough to live forever, too, Emerson thought, infuriated.

It was intolerable, living under the earl's thumb. Emerson wanted the roost to himself. But the old penny-pincher wouldn't die.

Well, Emerson was going to get his way in one matter at least. He was going to destroy Ravenswood. He was going to take Henrietta away from the viscount; devastate the man. And he was going to do it in front of the entire *ton*.

Emerson stormed into his bedroom.

The startled chambermaid shrieked.

Emerson eyed the feeble maid. He needed to feel in control. It burned inside him, the desire for power.

He slammed the door closed and advanced on the whimpering wench. With a rough movement, he grabbed her and tossed her onto the bed.

CHAPTER 28

Sebastian was at his wits end. He was getting married in two days and his bride still despised him. He needed help—and he could think of only one woman in the world who could give it to him.

A door in the wall opened from across the room.

Sebastian quirked a brow.

Very theatrical.

Madam Jacqueline entered the room. She was dressed in a white turban and flowing wrapper. Jewels sparkled from her ears, her wrinkled neckline, and her slender fingers.

She moved with grace and confidence, her steps dainty and refined. She impersonated womanly charm. But Sebastian didn't doubt she could be cruel—if she wanted to be. One didn't become the most notorious courtesan in England by being meek. One had to be shrewd and devious.

It bothered Sebastian to think that the innocent Miss Ashby had come to the ruthless woman for help—and all because she'd wanted to seduce him. He was only grateful the cunning courtesan had not destroyed the imprudent chit.

"Lord Ravenswood." She smiled. "I'm surprised by your visit."

"Are you, Madam Jacqueline? I wonder if perhaps you've been expecting me for quite some time?"

There was a gleam of pleasure in the woman's eyes, a smirking glow that was hard to ignore. She had immense affluence. But for all her wealth, her links to royalty, she had no blue blood in her veins. It infuriated her, he reckoned, to have so much power but be denied one critical thing: lineage. She had to enjoy having the aristocracy come to her for help. It must give her a sense of accomplishment and pride, vengeance even.

"Tea, my lord?"

"No, thank you."

Madman Jacqueline poured herself a steaming cup. She reclined in the divan and perused him with enchanting green eyes.

Sebastian could see why the woman commanded the attention of kings and gentlefolk alike. She had a mesmerizing quality about her.

"To what do I owe the honor of your visit, Lord Ravenswood?"

He took in a deep breath. "I presume you've heard about my wedding to Miss Ashby?"

She sipped her tea with feminine poise. "Yes, I read the announcement in the broadsheets. Congratulations."

"Thank you," he said stiffly. It was deuce uncomfortable having to ask the woman for assistance. But pride be damned. He had to figure out some way to get Henrietta to be his *wife*. She didn't want to live with him. She didn't want to touch him. How was he supposed to put up with that for the rest of his days? "I believe you offered Miss Ashby some advice—on how to seduce me."

"I did indeed, my lord."

"Well, I need some advice in return."

The woman lifted a painted brow. "How can I be of help?"

He shifted in his seat. "How do I seduce Miss Ashby?"

It was a very subtle quirk of the lips. "I beg your pardon, my lord?"

"You heard me," he growled.

"But you are engaged to marry the girl."

"Yes, but the stubborn chit doesn't want anything to do with me anymore."

"Really?" The courtesan was amused. How she must take pleasure in his discomfiture! "And why is that, my lord?"

"She doesn't trust me," he said, disgruntled.

"Why?"

"Because she discovered I'm a scoundrel."

"I see." Another sip of tea. "Have you offered her diamonds?"

Sebastian shot out of his chair and stalked about the room. "Madam Jacqueline, I think we both know I'm not some sort of innocent fawn. I've bedded the girl, offered her gifts, saved her from drowning, and *still* she wants nothing to do with me."

Madam Jacqueline raised a brow again. "Impressive."

"What do I do now?" he growled.

The courtesan set her teacup aside and folded her hands in her lap. "It sounds like the girl does not love you anymore."

There was something very striking about that word: "anymore." It implied Henrietta had once loved him but didn't care about him any longer. The realization was … crushing. Whenever Henrietta had looked at him in the past, he had *felt* noble, even heroic. It was hard to admit but Henrietta's faith in him had always been a comfort, an inspiration even. He forgot about his immoral ways when he was with her. He forgot about his loneliness. He felt only …

"What do you want, my lord?"

Sebastian looked at the courtesan, his reflection shattered. "I told you. How do I seduce Miss Ashby?"

"Why do you want to seduce her? Do you want Miss Ashby to adore you again? Or do you want her to love you for who you really are?"

Love him for who he really was? A scoundrel? "She will never love me for who I really am."

"And who are you, my lord?"

He took in a deep breath. "A villain."

The courtesan cocked her head. "Perhaps you should change your ways."

"I can't change my ways."

"And why not?"

"Because once a rogue, always a rogue."

She tsked. "Miss Ashby was once naïve. She's not anymore. People do change, my lord."

"Yes, all thanks to you," he grumbled.

"You don't like the change in Miss Ashby? You'd rather she worshiped you?"

"No." He grabbed the back of a chair. "I suppose I'd rather she loved me."

And he did. He didn't want Henrietta's blind adoration. He didn't want another warm body in his bed. He wanted the woman to be his wife. He wanted her to understand him, to comfort him, to care for him. And he wanted to do the same for her.

"Do you love her?" asked Madam Jacqueline

Did he? Could he? Or was he afraid, like Peter had suggested? Afraid of failing Henrietta. Afraid of not being a man worthy of her affection?

"I don't know," he admitted.

"Then I suppose the question is: can the girl love you? Does she still love you?"

Sebastian was in turmoil. There was so much revelation, so much truth pouring into his soul. He didn't know what to make of it all. "How do I find out?"

"If the girl's as stubborn as you say, I don't know that you can. Perhaps you should resign yourself to your fate?"

He gawked at her. "And this is your practical advice? Give up?"

"You have already tried everything. You said so yourself."

"But there must be *something* else I can do."

She lifted her eyes heavenward. "Well, there is one thing."

"What?"

She looked back at him. "You can die."

He glared at her. "You mock me."

"Not at all, my lord. You asked for my advice, and I've offered it."

"To die?"

"That's right."

Sebastian gnashed his teeth. "And just what would that accomplish—other than to put me out of my misery, of course?"

"Well, if the girl truly loves you, she will admit it once you are dead. You see, my lord, the will can be very strong to protect the heart. But dead, you do not threaten her heart anymore. She will let down her guard, and if she weeps over your corpse, she loves you."

Sebastian was beginning to think the woman's turban was wound too tight. "So I die, and Henrietta admits she loves me?"

"I'm afraid it's the only way to get the girl to confess her true feelings, my lord."

The old woman was daft. And Sebastian had wasted his time in coming to meet her.

"How enlightening, Madam Jacqueline. I thank you for your time."

She smiled. "Not at all, my lord."

Sebastian headed for the door in brisk strides.

"Lord Ravenswood?"

He paused. "Yes, Madam Jacqueline."

"When you see Miss Ashby again, please tell her I'm very proud of her."

Sebastian quit the room.

CHAPTER 29

Henrietta stood in front of the mirror and stared at her pink satin dress with lace trim. It was her wedding day. She was about to marry the man she had dreamed about for four long years. She was about to marry the man she had once loved for four long years. And she had never been so miserable.

Four emotional sisters gathered around her.

Penelope whispered, "You look so beautiful, Henry."

"Like an angel," confirmed Teria.

Cordelia sniffed. "I can't believe you're getting married."

"About time, too," from Roselyn.

Henrietta smiled at her sisters, though her spirit was heavy.

The bedroom door opened.

Henrietta looked over her shoulder. "Hullo, Mama."

The baroness stepped inside the room. "You look lovely, Henry."

"Doesn't she, Mama?" Penelope pinched the bride's cheeks to add some color. "A veritable princess."

The baroness nodded. "Ladies, I'd like a moment alone with my daughter."

The sisters bobbed their heads in obedience and cheerfully quit the room.

The baroness closed the door. "How do you feel, Henry?"

"Nervous," she admitted.

The older woman smiled. "I was nervous, too." She picked up the veil draped over the bed. "Here, let me help you with this."

Henrietta squatted, for Mama was a tad short.

The baroness artfully pinned the flowing white headdress to her hair, then picked up the crown of white roses. "And now for the finishing touch."

With a gentle stroke, Mama set the ring of flowers on her head.

Henrietta peered into the glass again, examining her polished appearance. It was almost time to make the wedding march. It was almost time to become the next Viscountess Ravenswood.

She was terribly queasy.

"I'd like to give you something, Henry."

"What is it, Mama?"

The baroness held up a sparkling floral brooch, facetted with rose pearls and diamonds. "My mother gave it to me on the day I married your father. I thought I would never part with it, but I'd like you to have it, Henry."

Henrietta eyed the brilliant gem and sniffed. "Thank you, Mama."

The baroness pinned the brooch at Henrietta's bust, the rose complimenting her dress. "Your father is waiting for you below stairs. He will escort you to the chapel."

"I'll be down in a minute, Mama."

The baroness kissed her cheek. "You will be happy, Henry."

She whispered, "How do you know, Mama?"

"Because I'm your mother; I know everything."

Henrietta smiled.

As soon as the baroness left the room, Henrietta searched for a kerchief. She rummaged through the accessories scattered across the vanity and pried a lacy napkin apart from the rest of the clutter.

She dabbed at her eyes. There was such tenderness in the expressions around her, such warmth. What a chilling contrast to the rogue she was set to marry in a matter of minutes!

A knock at the door.

Henrietta wiped her nose. "Come in."

She gasped. Sebastian stepped into the room, an achingly handsome sight in dapper blue togs. With a white waistcoat and gloves, he looked every inch the gentleman.

"What are you doing here?" she asked.

"I had to see you before the wedding." He dropped his sexy eyes to her toes and slowly lifted his gaze. "You look beautiful, Henry."

She shivered. "Thank you."

"Really, you look ravishing."

"Yes, I heard you."

A dashing smile. "I just wanted to make sure you believed me."

She pursed her lips. "What do you want, Sebastian?"

"To promise you I will make you happy. I won't grieve you the way my father grieved my mother."

She looked at him, baffled. "What about your parents?"

Henrietta didn't know very much about the former viscount and viscountess. Sebastian had never mentioned the couple.

"They didn't have a very good rapport," he said. "Father wasn't the best husband. He was distant, strict even. Not an easy man to love."

"What are you saying?"

"Will you give me a second chance to make you happy?"

Henrietta's heart fluttered. Was she willing to risk her heart to be with the viscount?

"Once a rogue, always a rogue," she said.

"People change, Henry … you did." He moved toward the door. "I'll be at the church."

Quietly he left the room.

Henrietta's wedding dress swished and swooshed as she paced the room. He'd asked her to give him a second chance, to trust him. Could she? Dare she?

She had changed, she thought. Dramatically. She'd wanted to change to be with Sebastian. Had he also changed? To be with her?

The hour of ten chimed somewhere in the house. It was time!

Henrietta rushed to the bed and grabbed her fur trimmed cape, scarf and gloves. She quickly quit the room and bustled toward the staircase.

But the whisper of voices from the landing below had her rooted to the spot.

"She's going to be late for her own wedding, Peter."

"Don't fuss, Penelope. We'll get her to the church on time."

"Oh, I still can't believe it, Peter! A prostitute?"

"Well, Seb was desperate," her husband hissed. "You know how much trouble he's been having with Henry"

"But to visit a woman of ill repute two days before his wedding? It's most unsavory."

A dizzy Henrietta grabbed the banister for support before she rolled down the stairs.

An ache filled her belly. She gasped for breath. Quickly she skirted across the hall before Peter and Penelope noticed her presence, and sprinted down the servant stairwell.

Tears filled her eyes. Sebastian was so "desperate" for a woman he'd seen a prostitute! And he'd promised never to go back to his vile club. She was such a fool. She had *almost* believed him when he'd asked for a second chance.

Henrietta pounded down the steps, surprising the cook in the kitchen. She brushed past the older woman and dashed through the scullery, buzzing with preparations for the wedding luncheon. Once she entered the main part of the house, she passed the dining hall and heard the sounds of clattering silverware—the table was being set for the guests—before making her way to the back of the house.

That fiend! He just couldn't keep his hands off a doxy, could he? It was in his blood, the wicked inclination to rut about with anything a skirt. And if she wasn't around to slake his lust, he'd find a whore to bed … and that's all she was to him, wasn't she? A harlot? All that rot about making her happy. The man only wanted one thing from her: carnal pleasure. He was an irredeemable rogue!

Henrietta sobbed as she ducked through the terrace doors. She took in a sharp breath to quell her sorrow.

She yanked on her gloves and sniffed. She deserved another broken heart. She always wavered over every decision. Even a sound one. She had marked Sebastian a rogue. And he was. A despicable rogue! So why had she even considered the idea that he could reform his ways?

It didn't matter anymore. This time she was *sure* Ravenswood was a rotten scoundrel. And she would not falter in her belief again. She might have to marry the bounder, but she did not have to let him near her heart again.

Henrietta had to get away from the house and all the merriment within its walls. The festive din was such a sharp contrast to her crushed spirit. She could not go to the church just yet. She needed to be alone.

"Miss Ashby."

Henrietta looked up, dazed. "Lord Emerson?"

Emerson had his hand tucked inside his breast pocket. "How delightful to see you."

She sniffed. "What are you doing here, my lord? Why aren't you at the church with the other guests?"

"I won't be attending the wedding, Miss Ashby … and neither will you."

He pulled out a pistol.

~ * ~

Sebastian stood beside the altar, waiting. It was just like Henrietta to be late for her own wedding.

The vicar flipped through the Bible, the pages snapping. The chapel, brimming with society's most fashionable members, was humming with idle chatter.

Sebastian girded himself for a long wait.

He reflected upon his earlier talk with Henrietta. Would she accept his offer to make her happy? He hoped so. He didn't want to spend the rest of his marital days in strife. And he wasn't desperate enough to prostrate his corpse at Henrietta's feet, as Madam Jacqueline had suggested.

But what if the chit rebuffed his offer?

It triggered a cramp in his chest, thinking about such a lonely existence. A ruthless irony, really. The girl had adored him for years; he could have snatched her up at any time. But now that he was going to marry her, she didn't want a fig to do with him.

Perhaps he was a villain, as Henrietta had said? Irredeemable, as his father had suggested? It would certainly explain all the trouble he'd been having, if he was damned to live a life apart from his wife.

Sebastian had to acknowledge the possibility. Maybe he just wasn't meant to be with Henrietta?

The chapel door burst opened. A breathless Peter stumbled inside. He righted himself quickly, smiled at the loquacious guests, and with brisk strides, marched down the aisle.

Sebastian growled, "Where is the bride, Peter?"

"There's been a snag, Seb."

"What sort of snag?"

"Why don't you come with me." The man's fixed smiled cracked. "Now."

Sebastian glowered at his brother. After a few whispered words to the vicar and a courteous nod to the guests, Sebastian strutted down the aisle after his brother.

As soon as he and his brother were clear of the chapel, Sebastian demanded, "What's happened, Peter?"

There were two horses waiting at the chapel, and both men mounted the beasts.

"It's Henry, Seb. She's missing."

Sebastian could feel the blood drain from his face. A cold darkness nestled in his belly, chilling his soul.

With a hard kick, he set the steed at a gallop.

CHAPTER 30

The house was in an uproar.

Sebastian and Peter stood under the doorframe, observing the commotion. The Ashby sisters either cried or argued. Husbands comforted wives. Children ran rampant. The servants bustled this way and that, fetching drinks, blankets … smelling salts?

Had someone fainted?

Sebastian stepped into the tumult. Peter closed the door.

The viscount scanned the front room, looking for Lady Ashby. But the baroness dashed into the foyer just then, a small bottle in her hand.

Who had fainted then?

Sebastian then noticed the unconscious baron slumped in a seat by the grandfather clock.

The baroness kneeled beside her husband and stuck the small bottle under his nose.

Within moments, the baron stirred, coughing and sputtering. "Gads, get that foul thing away from me!"

Sebastian demanded, "Where is Henry?"

"Oh God," the baron groaned. "Henry! Where's my Henry?"

Penelope stepped forward. "She's gone, Sebastian."

The viscount's breath hitched. "What do you mean 'gone'? Gone where?"

"She's … she's …"

Penelope, too distraught to answer, looked at her husband for support.

"She's run away, Seb," said Peter. He paused, then: "With another man."

Blood throbbed in Sebastian's head, howled in his ears. Henrietta had left him? Disgraced him at the altar in front of the *ton*?

"The other man's been courting her for a while, it seems," said Peter. "The butler remembers seeing him at the engagement party. The young lord also came to visit Henrietta after the accident on the ice."

It was crushing, the pressure on his chest. Sebastian couldn't breathe. All this time he had thought to woo Henrietta, to share a life with her … and she was having an affair. No wonder she'd rebuffed him at every turn. She had another lover!

He fisted his palms. The bile in his belly churned. Had she planned to humiliate him at the altar from the start of their engagement? Was this some sort of retaliation for breaking her girlhood dream?

"We have to go after her, Seb."

Sebastian swallowed the bitter taste in his mouth. "No, Peter."

Peter balked. "You're not serious, brother?"

"I am."

"But you love the girl, admit it!"

Sebastian snatched his brother's cravat. "I do not love Henrietta! Besides, the girl's made her choice, and I won't force her to change her mind."

Sebastian released his brother before he strangled the man. He wasn't angry with Peter. He was angry with himself.

Curse her! The scheming chit had made him *want* to be a better man. She had fooled him into thinking he had a chance at a future with her, that he wasn't damned after all.

What tripe! She and her lover must be roaring with laughter. And that was the greatest reprisal of all, getting the dim-witted viscount to think he'd had an opportunity at happiness. Had she and her paramour bandied that letter all over Town, too? Orchestrated the whole engagement just to devastate him?

Pain hacked his insides to mush.

"Seb, I know you're angry, but we have to go after the girl," Peter implored. "If nothing else, think of the Ashby name!"

A listless Sebastian said, "It's not the Ashby name that's ruined, it's mine."

"But she's run off with another man!"

"She's off to marry her lover, I'm sure. She'll be home in a few days, a beaming new bride from Gretna Green. The gossip will fizzle. It always does."

But the rancor in Sebastian's gut would never go away; it would haunt him all the rest of his miserable days.

Peter huffed, "It isn't right, Seb."

The baron groaned. "Oh, my darling Henry! What will I ever do without the boy?"

Lady Ashby fluttered a fan over her husband's flushed cheeks.

Peter nudged his brother. "Look at the baron, Seb. We have to do something for his sake."

Sebastian didn't like to see the baron in such distress, but Henrietta had made her choice. What right did he have to go after her?

"No, Peter."

"But the baron doesn't want the girl to wed another man."

"The baron doesn't want Henrietta to wed *any* man," said Sebastian. "Even me. But we both know the girl has to get married now."

Especially now that she might be enceinte.

Sebastian's heart pounded at the thought. The chit might be pregnant with his child. She *needed* a husband. She just didn't want him to play the parental role. Another man would raise his child. The image blanketed him in even greater despair.

"But we don't even know anything about this Emerson!" Peter cried.

Sebastian bristled. "Emerson?"

Peter nodded. "The butler said Lord Emerson had called on the girl, that the couple had dashed off together. He witnessed the two running across the green, hand in hand."

Sebastian tried to recall a scene from the Hellfire Club. It was a blurred vision, but he was sure there had been a row between him and Emerson—over Henrietta.

Hand in hand? A lover's elopement? Not bloody likely. Emerson had dragged her away—by force. The villain was not the sort of man to get leg-shackled. He might have charmed Henrietta, tricked her into thinking him a respectable sort, but he was nothing of the kind. He was a dastardly son of a bitch—and he had a taste for Sebastian's blood.

The letter! The rumor in the paper! It had to be Emerson's doing. All of it. Sebastian had been reading the letter when Emerson had interrupted him. The fiend must have snatched it from him after the fight, then aired it all over Town to get even with him. And according to the butler, Emerson had attended the engagement party. If he'd overheard Henrietta's confession, that she wanted a marriage in name only, *he* must have spread the tale in the society papers.

With brisk and determined strides, Sebastian thundered toward the door.

He could feel it, deep inside his gut. Emerson had taken Henrietta, kidnapped her to get back at him for some foolish quarrel. Sebastian couldn't even remember what they had squabbled about, but he knew Emerson a craven knave bent on petty retribution—and Sebastian knew just where the bastard had taken Henrietta.

"Where are you going, Seb?"

Peter sprinted to keep up with his brother's long strides.

"To fetch Henrietta back."

"Thank God!"

Sebastian mounted a horse. "*You* are not coming with me, brother."

"You can't go after the couple alone. You might need me, Seb."

"No!" Sebastian twisted the reins around his palms. "I want you to fetch the magistrate, Peter. Bring him to the Hellfire Club."

Peter paled. "Oh, good God. Seb, you have to let me—"

"No! It's too dangerous, Peter. You have a wife. I don't want you to come with me. I don't want you to risk your neck."

"Oh, blast it! Here, then." Peter reached behind his back. "You're going to need this."

A pistol appeared.

Sebastian eyed the piece. "Where did you get that?"

"From the baron. I figured Emerson might put up a fuss if we tried to bring the girl home. But I didn't think he was *that* dangerous."

Sebastian tucked the weapon into his waist.

"Be careful, Seb."

But Sebastian was already pounding the drive at breakneck speed.

CHAPTER 31

It was cold inside the abbey. Dank, too. Tears burned in Henrietta's eyes. Blood seeped from the wounds at her wrists, trussed with rope. But she didn't care. She thrashed against her dastardly captor, bit him, too.

Emerson hollered, "You bitch!"

He licked the wound at his finger, then slapped her soundly for imparting the injury. He grabbed her by the hair and shoved her down the dark passageway.

Bruised cheek throbbing, she gritted, "Why are you doing this?"

"Quiet, you little whore!"

It was clear the man loathed her, considered her a harlot. She didn't care for his good opinion of her, but she did care to know his motivation.

"It was *you* who flaunted my letter all over London, wasn't it? It was *you* who spread that dreadful rumor in the paper?"

"It was indeed."

"But why did you do it?"

"To avenge myself on Ravenswood."

There was a terrible ache in Henrietta's ear, a sort of buzzing sound. "How do you know Ravenswood? And how do you know about the Hellfire Club?"

"Don't feign innocent with me," he sneered. "We all three frequent the club."

Henrietta gasped. Another cold chill gripped her. And this time it was not the winter air making her shiver.

"Oh, yes, I know what you are, you strumpet. I saw you with Ravenswood in the catacombs right after you stomped on my foot."

She remembered a man in a mask—wanting to strap her to the banquet table for an orgy.

Henrietta had a profound urge to retch. "So you're a member of the Hellfire Club, too?"

"*Was* a member before your lover humiliated me in front of the friars. But Ravenswood will pay for what he did to me. He took my pride from me, so I'm going to take something from him. *You*."

She shuddered under his biting words. "What do you mean?"

"Stop yapping!"

Henrietta was forced down the stone steps into the catacombs. She trembled. The brisk air nipped at her nose. It was dark inside the catacombs: a torch here or there. It was noisy, too, the rowdy din of merry "friars" echoing throughout the tunnel.

She closed her eyes to bring her thundering heartbeats to a steadier canter. "If you're a former member of the club, what are we doing here?"

"I'm going to avenge myself on Ravenswood *and* win back the respect of the friars. And you are going to help me do it."

"You can go to the devil, Emerson. I won't help you!"

She jabbed her elbow into his ribs.

He grimaced—and tightened his grip.

"I've never met such a fussy slut," he growled.

Emerson tore the neck cloth from his throat and gagged her.

Henrietta choked on her tears. She stumbled through the chilling channel, pushed to the arena's threshold.

Inside the banquet hall, she spied the notorious banquet table—and the shackles at the table's edges.

Her heart shuddered.

"Emerson!" the friars jeered. The room was filled with heckling villains, wenches, too, all foxed and loving it. "Did you run off to get married?"

The cackles must have burned Emerson's blood, for Henrietta could feel him bristle behind her.

Emerson growled, "She's not my bride, brothers … she's ours."

The inebriated friars piqued at the implication.

Emerson pushed her toward the table. Henrietta screamed against her gag and kicked, letting loose a savage tantrum. But it was futile. The drunken carousers grabbed her wrists, her ankles and hoisted her onto the banquet table.

She kicked again, but Emerson gripped her ankles, spread her legs apart. He secured the manacles at her boots. Some other foul oaf wrested her bound wrists and clipped the heavy irons above her head.

There was a throbbing pressure on her breast, as her heart pumped hard and fast. She flicked her eyes across the room in dashing strokes, searching for help, for some way out. But she was trapped.

Emerson moved to the head of the table. He looked at her with venom, and whispered, "Once the friars feast on you, I'll be accepted back into the club, and Ravenswood will be devastated. Your pain will be his." Emerson stepped back and smiled. "Who has a dagger, brothers? Let's tear this dress to pieces and enjoy our bride."

A glittering blade appeared.

Henrietta thrashed against her bonds.

"Don't fight too much." Emerson winked. "It'll only hurt more."

A pistol cocked.

Henrietta stiffened … but then her heart throbbed with unfettered joy.

Ravenswood!

The viscount stepped into the catacombs, covered in snow. He was a wonderful sight! The exertion of a pounding ride was evident in his body. He had come for her. She wasn't alone in the chilling darkness of the abbey anymore, trapped with a band of devils. The relief inside her was overwhelming. The joy almost crippling.

Sebastian approached the table, murder in his eyes. "Let her go."

The friars slowly backed away.

A flabbergasted Emerson quickly gathered his wits and released her.

Henrietta yanked the neck cloth out of her mouth and let out a desperate sob.

"Come here, Henry," Sebastian ordered, gun still trained on a dastardly Emerson.

She took one shaky step, then two. But before she could reach the viscount, Emerson pulled a pistol from his coat and jerked her roughly into his embrace. He coiled his arm around her throat and placed the pistol at her temple.

"I'm going to have my revenge, Ravenswood."

Henrietta could feel the earth spinning again. Revenge? On Ravenswood?

"Stop right there, Ravenswood," cried Emerson, "or I'll kill her where she stands!"

Sebastian stilled.

"Drop the pistol, Ravenswood!"

Emerson clearly didn't want to give the viscount an opportunity to shoot him. And Ravenswood didn't hesitate.

Cold metal hit the stone floor and resounded throughout the catacombs.

Henrietta wanted to scream, but Emerson's hold over her neck prevented the outcry. Unarmed, Ravenswood was a clear mark. She thrashed instead.

"Hold still!" barked Emerson. "Do you want me to squeeze the trigger by mishap?"

"Be still, Henry," Sebastian snapped.

She went very still.

Something snagged on her heart at the sight of Sebastian, an ache so profound she gasped for breath. She didn't know what the sentiment was; she had never felt such a crushing pressure before. But to see him standing there. To know that he was in danger …

"You just had to take everything from me, didn't you?" said Emerson.

Even though Ravenswood was defenseless, Emerson still trembled. Henrietta could feel him quivering against her backside.

"Don't be a fool," growled Sebastian. "I didn't take anything from you."

The villain snorted. "I suppose my pride *is* nothing to you, isn't it?"

"What are you talking about?"

"The friars all think me a coward."

Sebastian looked confused. "Why?"

"Because you chased me under the table when I suggested we have this wench for our next banquet. I was a laughing stock! Don't you remember?"

"I was foxed, Emerson."

"Well, I remember. I was going to make everything right tonight, but you had to take *that* away from me, too. I'm going to make you suffer for what you did to me, Ravenswood."

Emerson lifted the pistol from Henrietta's temple and pointed it at Ravenswood instead.

Henrietta kicked back her boot and slammed it into Emerson's shin.

He yelped and tossed her aside.

She hit the ground.

Sebastian started toward her, but Emerson regained his balance and steadied the pistol. He aimed the weapon once more at the viscount's chest.

Henrietta grabbed the pistol Ravenswood had cast aside, and in a sweeping gesture, her wrists still bound, she cocked the gun, aimed, and shot the pistol clear out of Emerson's grip.

Both men looked stunned.

Sebastian quirked a brow at her. "You really are a good shot, aren't you, Henry?"

Henrietta sobbed again.

Emerson screamed. He hit the ground, frantic to find his pistol: his only means of protection against Ravenswood's wrath.

But it did no good.

Ravenswood grabbed him and trounced him soundly: a solid jab to the midriff.

Emerson keeled over, sputtering.

"I'm going to let the magistrate deal with you," snarled Sebastian. "I'm going to enjoy watching you hang."

Ravenswood picked up the villain's gun and walked away. There was no reason to hurt the feeble creature anymore.

Henrietta scrambled to her feet and rushed out of the banquet hall.

Sebastian shouted, "Henry!"

But she didn't stop. She had to get out of the catacombs, away from the abbey. She stumbled up the winding stairs, darted through the dark passageway and burst out into the cold night air.

She tossed Papa's pistol into the snow, brought her shivering fingers to her face—and wailed.

"Henry, are you all right?"

A warm and comforting set of arms wrapped around her.

She stuck out her wrists. "U-untie me."

Sebastian unfastened the knot at her wrists, kissed her bloody wounds before he bound the injuries with strips from his neck cloth.

Something thunderous resounded in the distance.

"W-who's that?" she said with shaky breath.

Two figures on horseback were fast approaching, the horses' hooves kicking up snow in wild stomps.

"It's Peter and the magistrate. You're safe, Henry." Ravenswood caressed her bruised and tender cheek. "That miserable bastard!"

She jerked her face away. "I-I'll be all right. Please take me home."

Sebastian glowered. "Henry, what is it?"

Wretched tears! It was so hard to find her voice between sobs. "I just want to forget about everything that happened today."

He looked stricken. "Henry … did Emerson force himself on you?"

"No!" She wiped the briny drops from her eyes. "Stop being so wonderful, Sebastian! Stop acting like a gentleman! I can't take the lies anymore."

He grabbed her by the shoulders, rankled. "Damn it, Henry—"

"I know you went to see a doxy," she cried. "You haven't changed one little bit!"

He let her go then, raked a shaky hand through his tousled curls. "You're right. I did go to see a prostitute."

She shuddered. "You're not even going to try to deny it?"

"I went to see Madam Jacqueline, you foolish chit!"

Henrietta hiccupped. "The courtesan? But why?"

"Because I needed her advice. I didn't know how else to get you to trust me." He sighed. "You're bloody stubborn, Henry. When are you going to realize that I'm not the same man you stumbled upon in the Hellfire Club?"

Henrietta looked deep into Sebastian's eyes, so hot. He radiated a noble strength—a truth—even amid the cold and dead of winter.

He grouched, "And Madam Jacqueline has a message for you."

Disarmed by the intensity of what she was feeling, Henrietta squeaked, "What is it?"

"She wants me to tell you that she's proud of you for so thoroughly bewitching me."

For some absurd reason, Henrietta simpered at the words.

"Henry." Sebastian lifted his hand and traced his forefinger softly across her cheek. "You vixen, I—"

"You son of bitch!"

Henrietta gasped.

A weak Emerson staggered out of the abbey, eyes burning with an unquenchable hatred for Ravenswood. He snatched the pistol Henrietta had discarded in the snow, lifted it—and aimed it straight at her. "I want you to live with pain, Ravenswood."

Ravenswood twisted his body around her and roared, "*No!*"

The shot ripped through the quiet countryside, echoing.

Henrietta screamed.

Ravenswood hit the snow, so still.

"Sebastian!"

On her knees, a tearful Henrietta hovered over the wounded viscount.

The snow was steeped in blood. She could feel the sticky liquid between her gloved fingers. Sebastian had stepped in front of the bullet to shield her. He had saved her life—again!

A frantic Henrietta patted his body, searching for the wound.

The magistrate appeared, Peter fast on his heels. The men dismounted and quickly tackled Emerson to the ground, confiscating the weapon.

But it was too late to help Sebastian.

Henrietta pounded on Sebastian's chest. "Wake up!"

But Sebastian didn't move. He wasn't breathing, either.

A tremendous grief swallowed her heart and spirit: a boundless misery sucked her into a chasm of darkness.

She crumpled on top of Sebastian and let out a sorrowful sob, wanting to die right there beside him. He had changed his wicked ways for her. He had told her so himself, but she hadn't believed him.

Guilt weighed in her belly. It was bitter to taste. She was going to suffer for her stubbornness. She was going to spend the rest of her days alone—without Sebastian. Oh God!

"I knew you loved me, Henry."

Henrietta hardened.

Slowly she lifted her head and looked down at Sebastian. She noted the sensuous smile even through her tears.

"Why you miserable"—she struck him—"wretched"—she struck him again—"rogue! Did you just *play* dead?"

Sebastian grabbed her and hoisted her until she was straddled across his lap.

"Tell me you love me, Henry."

"I'd rather eat worms!"

He grabbed her cheeks and yanked her to his lips—or a hair's breadth away. Oh, sweet heaven, it felt so good to be this close to him again!

"Tell me you love me, Henry."

Henrietta looked deep into the rogue's dashing blue eyes—and kissed him. She crushed her lips over his until he couldn't breathe.

"I love you," she whispered. And kissed him again. "I love you. I love you. I love you."

Sebastian chuckled between kisses and gave her a tight hug. "I love you too, Henry. I don't know when it crept up on me, but I think I've loved you for a while … And I always will."

Henrietta was weeping again. But for a whole other reason. The fear in her heart was gone. She trusted Sebastian. She *loved* Sebastian. Really loved him. For years she had nursed a girlhood fantasy. She had been smitten with a dream. But now she knew Sebastian's true nature … and it was more wonderful than she had imagined. He wasn't perfect—neither was she—but he was her *im*perfect hero. And she loved every bit of him.

"Uh-um."

"What do you want, Peter?" growled Sebastian. "Can't you see I'm engaged at the moment?"

"Yes, well, I was going to offer to dress that wound in your arm, but if you'd rather bleed to death …?"

Henrietta gasped. "Your wound!"

She quickly groped along his arm and fingered the blood.

"It's nothing," said Sebastian. "A graze."

"Still." Henrietta struggled to get off his lap. "We have to get you to a doctor."

Henrietta quickly stripped the scarf from her throat and wrapped it around his injury.

"I see I'm not needed." A chuckling Peter returned his attention to the magistrate and Emerson.

"Well, Henry, I suppose there's only one thing left to do," said Sebastian.

Henrietta was busy ministering to the viscount's injury, so she furled her brow and said, "I'll have the wound stitched up in a second."

"Not that, Henry." He took her by the hands and kissed her knuckles. "You still have to consent to be my wife—in every way."

A brow lifted. "Oh, do I now?"

"Henry," he growled.

With a wicked smile, Henrietta slipped her arms around Sebastian. "Kiss me and I'll think about it."

And he kissed her: a wild, sensuous, heart-stopping kiss.

As if she'd ever give *that* up for the rest of her days.

EPILOGUE

Henrietta dawdled the baby on her knees.

"He has Peter's nose," she said, inspecting the infant's profile. "Don't you think so, Sebastian?"

The viscount shrugged. "I suppose so."

Henrietta looked at her husband, sprawled in an armchair, legs stretched and crossed at the ankles. He was like a lazy cat, perusing his surroundings.

"Something else on your mind, my lord?"

He grinned at the appellation, a term of endearment now. "I'm just admiring the sight of you, my lady."

Henrietta snorted.

She lifted the baby to her lips and kissed him on the nose. "Your uncle Seb is such a rogue. How shall we punish him, Frederick?"

Frederick gurgled in his aunt Henry's arms.

"Lock him out of the bedroom, you say?" She grinned. "What a wonderful idea."

Sebastian chuckled.

Peter sauntered into the room just then, and beamed to see his son. "How is the dear boy?"

Henrietta handed the fussing babe over to his Papa. "A darling, Peter. As ever."

The proud father settled into the settee, and propped the infant across his chest. "He is a dear, isn't he? Handsome, too. Although I think he has your nose, Seb."

Sebastian rolled his eyes.

Henrietta fell back in her chair with laughter. She was so very happy for her sister and Peter. Little Frederick was a much sought-after addition to the family.

Henrietta sighed, content with the idle autumn day. The family had gathered again at Baron Ashby's country home. Poor Papa had been very sorry to see the last of his offspring marry and leave the nest. But Henrietta had made a promise to visit often. The whole family had made the same vow, much to the baroness's displeasure. Mama was not one to suffer a house filled with noisy children. But for the sake of the baron's good cheer, Mama reluctantly endured the reunions.

Henrietta nestled in her chair and gazed at her husband with love. How she adored the man! It filled her heart with such joy, being with her reformed rogue.

The dastardly Emerson had been exiled to Australia. His father, the Earl of Ormsby, happened to wield enough clout to spare his wretched son from the gallows. Even though the earl did not get along with his son, he couldn't let the villain hang. Blood was blood. Or so Henrietta had heard. She didn't trouble herself with such details. Life in a penal colony was a much more fitting form of punishment, she was sure. All she really cared about was her family—and her darling husband.

A crash resounded through the house, followed by the squeals of children.

Sebastian sighed. "Too many babies."

Peter chuckled at that. "And when will *you*, dear brother, become a father?"

Sebastian made a moue in jest. "Why would I want to do that? Now that you have a son, Peter, I don't need an heir."

"I think your wife might have something to say about that."

Sebastian looked at his wife.

Henrietta quirked a brow. She had yet to have a babe … but she was determined to change all that.

"No babies, my lord?" she said.

Sebastian pretended to think about it—then a slow and wolfish smile touched his lips. "Well, maybe one brat."

Peter cradled the babe and pounced to his feet. "Come along, Frederick. I don't think you need to hear this."

Father and son quickly vacated the room.

Alone with her husband, Henrietta put all her seductive training to good use, and crossed the rug in very sensual strides.

Sebastian followed her ever move with avid interest.

She settled comfortably on his lap and traced her forefinger along the ridge of his masculine jaw. "Just one babe, my lord?"

He wrapped his arms tight around her waist. "Well, maybe two."

Henrietta giggled and kissed him with passion. Breathless, she said, "And when will we start to try for this babe or two?"

"How does right now sound?"

She nipped at his lush lip. "It sounds very agreeable."

She grabbed his hand.

"A minute, Henry."

"What is it?"

"Do you still have that naughty book of pictures?"

She pinched her brows. "Yes ..."

"Perhaps we should draw inspiration from the book?"

She let out a smoky laugh. "What a wonderful idea, my lord!"

END

ABOUT THE AUTHOR

ALEXANDRA BENEDICT is the author of several historical romance novels. Her work has received critical acclaim from Booklist and a rare and coveted starred review from Publishers Weekly. Romantic Times awarded her a "Top Pick" review and raved: "There is nothing quite as exciting as finding a fresh, vibrant new voice, and Benedict has it!" All of Alexandra's books are translated into various languages. To learn more visit: **www.AlexandraBenedict.ca** or like her on **FACEBOOK** at Alexandra Benedict Author.

Printed in Great Britain
by Amazon

23534967R00129